The Case of the Stolen Pink Tombstone

A Witch's Cove Mystery
Book 16

Vella Day

A scary night. A really weird theft. And some very unexpected helpers—or not so helpful helpers.

Picture this: Halloween night at the cemetery. Full moon with fog creeping along the ground mixed with the intermittent sound of owls. Scary, right? It was nothing compared to what was to happen next.

Hi, I'm Glinda Goodall, part owner of the Pink Iguana Sleuths, and I'm not afraid of death. Heck, my parents own the town's funeral home. But when someone takes the pink granite tombstone of one of the town's richest widows, I can't help but wonder what kind of evil person or being did this.

After a trail of dead ends, the sheriff asks me and my partner to help. I hoped I'd finally get a simple case, but boy was I wrong—again. That is until a very chatty and pompous white cat does a tell all. Okay, some gargoyle shifters had a hand in solving this case, too.

If you want to keep up-to-date on the progress, ask my pink familiar, Iggy the iguana—but that's assuming you're a witch. Otherwise, you can't understand him. Or just drop by our office and I'll sit and chat.

Chapter One

I'D JUST SAT down on the sofa when Penny Carsted, my best friend, breezed in through the office door, carrying a bottle of wine. Not that Penny didn't often arrive with a gift when we had our girls' night, but she certainly didn't come to the office with wine at three thirty in the afternoon.

Adding to the strangeness was that she'd come from her waitressing job. How could I tell? Penny was still wearing her uniform, which was a skirt covered in pennies. Why pennies? Because my Aunt Fern, who owned the Tiki Hut Grill, required every staff member to wear a costume. I know this, because I used to work there before starting up the Pink Iguana Sleuths with my now fiancé, Jaxson Harrison. Back then, I wore a pink Glinda the Good Witch outfit—but that's a story for another time.

"This is a nice surprise," I said.

She grinned. "I come bearing gifts."

"I can see that." I had no idea what the occasion was. "Have a seat and tell me what's going on." My mouth dropped open when a possibility struck. "You and Hunter got engaged."

She waved her free hand and sat down next to me. "No. We're not like you and Jaxson. We need more time. Besides, I have Tommy to think about. I don't want to confuse him by having his dad there part time and also have it be official between me and Hunter."

"I can understand that." Tommy was her nine-year old son. I nodded to the wine bottle in her hand. "So what is the occasion?"

"I need a favor."

I chuckled. "You didn't need to give me a gift for that. Or do you need the Pink Iguana Sleuths' talents to solve some crime?"

She laughed. "It's nothing like that. Today, I got a call from Tommy's school."

That usually wasn't good. I sobered. "Did something happen?"

"Not exactly, other than one of the mothers who promised to help out with the Halloween Haunted Cemetery night for the third graders got sick, and I need a replacement."

Uh-oh. I could connect the dots. "You know I love our cemetery, and you thought I'd be the perfect person to chaperone a bunch of kids. Is that it?"

"Yes. We'd have fun, and you'd be great!" Her eyes widened. The huge intake of breath implied she was hoping I'd say yes. The problem was that I could never say no to Penny, and she knew it.

"Why would I be good?" This should be interesting.

"You must have a bunch of spooky tales to tell. After all, your parents run the funeral home."

That had nothing to do with anything, but I didn't need to argue. "When does this event take place?"

"I knew you'd say yes. It's tomorrow night from eight

until nine."

Halloween was on Sunday. "The administration picked Friday because the kids don't have school the next day?"

"Exactly. So, you'll do it?"

"Of course, and I'll even see if I can drag Jaxson with me."

"That's even better. Hunter said he'd try to make it if he can get out of going to some meeting."

On a Friday night? It was possible roaming around a cemetery might not be his thing.

"Perfect. The men can hang out and keep us safe while we try to maintain some control over the kiddies." A very bizarre image crossed my mind. "You know, since Hunter is a wolf shifter, he could roam the cemetery in his animal form and really scare the kids."

Yes, I was kidding, but it would have been fun to see the children's reaction.

"Aren't you the funny one. First of all, Hunter would never do that, and secondly, the kids are nine-years-old. I don't want them scarred for life." She leaned forward. "One of the parents agreed to dress up in a sheet and pretend to be a ghost. That's about as far as I'm willing to take it."

I chuckled. "I thought you didn't want to traumatize the poor kids."

She waved a hand. "If anyone cries, I'll tell them the truth."

Not only did I love old cemeteries, my nineteen-year old cousin who was in school studying photography loved Hamilton Cemetery even more. "Maybe I can ask Rihanna to come along. She loves going there. I don't know if she's been at night, but whether she has or hasn't, she might want to take pictures."

"Hunter and I were able to check it out last week. They have lights randomly placed throughout the grounds, I guess to prevent people from tripping over any tombstones. Rihanna can even snap pictures without her flash."

"That sounds good, but I thought the cemetery was closed at night."

"Oh yeah, it is, so I'm not sure why they'd need lights, unless they need them for the cameras—assuming they have them. I mean, I would. Some people might want to climb over the fence and walk around the dead at night." She waved a hand. "All I know, is that the cemetery will be open until nine for the next few days in honor of Halloween."

"Good to know." I stood. "Let me get a bottle opener and some glasses so we can celebrate properly."

"You don't have to drink this now, you know."

I rarely drank, and I certainly didn't drink during the day, but what the heck. "Why not? I have nothing to do. Jaxson is working on the monkey bridge, and we have no cases. We'll stick to one glass."

She giggled. "Drinking in the afternoon is decadent."

"It is. To limit the effects, let me find something to snack on."

I stepped into the makeshift kitchen and grabbed two wine glasses and a corkscrew, along with a bag of cookies. No sooner had I set them on the coffee table when Jaxson returned carrying Iggy.

"How did it go with supervising the installation of the monkey bridge?" I know we had no monkeys in Witch's Cove, Florida, but we had squirrels, cats, maybe some rats, and definitely one very determine iguana who wanted to cross the busy main street while staying out of harm's way.

"It was a success," Jaxson said.

"It's awesome," my nine-pound pink iguana chimed in.

"What exactly is a monkey bridge, and where is it going to be?" Penny asked.

"I'll let Jaxson give you the lowdown since he and Iggy were instrumental in getting it set up. Jaxson, while you give Penny the details, do you mind opening the bottle for us while I grab you a glass?"

"Certainly. What are you celebrating?"

"I'll tell you after you give us the details of Iggy's big adventure."

While he opened the wine, I rushed into the kitchen. As I was retrieving a wine glass for him, Jaxson explained what a monkey bridge was to Penny. We needed to celebrate the long-awaited bridge that would allow Iggy to go from our office to the row of buildings on the other side. His best friend—a mute gargoyle shifter—mostly resided in the Hex and Bones Apothecary, which was where I purchased the ingredients for any spells I did. And yes, I am a witch, which is why I have a familiar—a very chatty talking pink iguana.

When I returned, Jaxson poured us each a small glass.

"Can I have a taste?" Iggy asked.

"Of wine? No. You're too young. Plus, I don't think you'd like wine."

"Let me decide for myself."

"Ask me again in a few years."

"You're no fun."

Maybe not, but I was trying to be a responsible parent.

Someday, Jaxson and I would have human children to raise.

I lifted my glass. "To Iggy safely crossing the street."

"It's not finished yet." Iggy dropped down onto his stomach.

I looked over at Jaxson. "When will it be done?"

"Either later today or by tomorrow morning. Just in time for Iggy to watch all of the Halloween festivities from his sacred little bridge."

I didn't like the idea of him being above the traffic in case the bridge gave way. "Are you sure that little piece of string will hold up?" I'd seen the bridge before it was installed. It was about six inches wide and was made of green mesh. The bridge had sides, preventing Iggy from falling off, but no telling how well it was tied at both ends.

"Don't worry. I don't plan to sit up there," Iggy said. "I'll be a target for you know who."

I chuckled, because Iggy's nemesis was a white seagull who had black tipped wings who he'd dubbed, Tippy. Being a typical seagull, he had a tendency to poop at random—or at not so random—times. "That's smart."

"I promise it won't fall into disrepair. I'll make sure the city maintains it," Jaxson said.

"Thank you." I believed him. He loved Iggy as much as I did. Not only that, we'd donated some money to the city to keep the bridge maintained. I was the only one with an iguana so I doubted anyone but Iggy would use it, unless the other animals figured out what it was for.

"Tell me what you and Penny are celebrating," Jaxson said.

"I came to bribe Glinda into joining me tomorrow night

at the elementary school's Halloween Haunted Cemetery walk. At night. Spooky, huh? We'll even have a parent dressed up as a ghost to scare the kids. It will be perfect."

Jaxson looked at me. "You agreed?"

"Sure. It'll be fun to see how the kids react. I know a few ghost stories I could tell."

Jaxson shook his head. "Poor kids."

Iggy crawled up onto the coffee table. "I want to go."

"No. It is at night, and the kids might step on you."

He looked up at Jaxson. "Tell her I'll stay in her purse."

Why didn't he ask me? "What are you afraid of, Iggy? That Tippy will come through that cat door and poop on you if we're not here?"

He scurried off the table so fast, all I saw was a blur. I really hadn't meant to frighten him. Poor guy.

"Glinda," Jaxson said.

"Yes?"

"I'll carry him."

Sometimes it wasn't worth the argument. "That works, too."

Iggy didn't emerge from under the sofa, but that was okay. He needed to come to grips with his fear of seagulls—or rather one particular seagull.

Penny finished her wine and then stood. "I need to go, but how about meeting us at the school at seven forty-five?"

"It's a date."

I hugged her goodbye, and once she left, I turned to Jaxson. "You're okay with this?"

"Of course. Besides, Iggy might have fun, if he doesn't get *scared*." The last word was said much louder than the others.

My familiar finally peeked his head out from under the sofa. "Me? Scared?"

"You do know that seagulls fly at night, don't you?" I wasn't trying to dissuade him, but if he got loose, it could be a problem.

"I'm not dumb, though I think I'll stay in your bag just to be safe. I'm only going so I can hear the little kids shriek when that parent jumps out at them."

"You do that."

I'd just placed the wine glasses in the sink when Rihanna came home from junior college.

"You just missed Penny," I said.

"She was here? What did she want?"

I told her about my exciting Friday night. "You're welcome to join us. I thought you might want to take pictures."

"That sounds fabulous. I've been to Hamilton Cemetery tons of times, but only during the day. Tomorrow night, you said?"

"Yes."

"Are you dressing up?"

"I hadn't thought that far ahead. Aunt Fern isn't doing her usual annual event because of what happened last year, so I didn't pick up another costume." I turned to Jaxson. "You up for a little costume shopping?"

"I have nothing to wear, so sure. And since we did just rent out the empty store across the street to a costume shop, I'm sure I can find something."

"Great!"

"What will you go as?" Rihanna asked.

Last year I went as Supergirl so that Jaxson could be Superman. "I'm not sure. Since it is a cemetery, maybe I should go as the grim reaper."

"That's what I was going to go as," Rihanna said. I couldn't tell if she was disappointed that we would match, or if she was excited we'd be a pair.

"Maybe it would be cool if all three of us went as grim reapers." I sounded like a geek, I know.

She studied me. "Fine, as long as you wear a pink ribbon on your chest."

"Why? Because I always wear pink?" Or almost always.

She rolled her eyes like only a teenager could do. "The pink means that you get to take the souls of the pure people."

I laughed. "You made that up."

"Okay, maybe I did."

I looked up at Jaxson. "You good with this?"

"Anything for you, but I can't imagine there will be a lot of costumes left in the store. Halloween is in three days."

He usually wasn't this pessimistic. "We won't know unless we ask. Besides, I imagine Mr. Mortimer will be happy to have the business."

Jaxson nodded to Iggy. "What about smaller sizes?"

"He can wear his Tippy-proof cape."

My Aunt Fern had recently made him one to protect Iggy when he went outside. This panicked request by my familiar happened after one of the local seagulls began tormenting poor Iggy. Of late, he hadn't been wearing it, but he still had it.

"Sounds good. Want to check it out now?" Jaxson said.

I looked over at Rihanna whose closet was comprised of mostly black clothes. She didn't need to buy a grim reaper outfit. "Care to join us?"

"Sure, I'd love to see what this new place carries."

"Me, too." Even though Jaxson and I had purchased the strip of stores across the street after receiving a windfall from our most bizarre case, Jaxson and our lawyers had done the transaction with Mr. Mortimer. I'd yet to meet the owner.

Chapter Two

"WE'RE GOING ON a school bus?" Rihanna asked.

"So it seems." I honestly wasn't sure why I expected we'd drive ourselves. Someone had to watch the kids. "We are the chaperones, after all."

Some third grader tugged on Jaxson's arm. "What are you supposed to be, mister?"

I almost laughed. Poor Jaxson. To the dismay of the new owner, Mr. Mortimer, none of the costumes at the store had been in Jaxson's size, so my fiancé went with a black suit and a black T-shirt. I thought the rake handle with the rubber-shaped scythe was a nice touch.

"I'm the grim reaper."

"You look more like an undertaker."

Jaxson smiled. "You might be right. You're going to be brave, tonight, right?" he asked the young man.

"There's nothing to be scared about. It's just a bunch of dead people here."

He was right about that. "What if we did a séance and some of the ghosts come out of their graves? Would that be fun?" And no, I wasn't serious.

"Yes! Can we?"

"Have you ever seen a ghost?"

"No, but I'd like to."

Few people could see ghosts. I was one of the chosen ones, however. "If they have some candles lying around the cemetery, maybe we can do one. Now go on. Get on the bus."

"Okay."

Unfortunately, Hunter wasn't able to get away from his work commitment. To say the least, I was disappointed, and I'm sure both Jaxson and Penny were too.

Once Penny gave us the go ahead to board the bus, we stepped inside, and memories of field trips came flooding back. Like always, the kids seemed to have migrated to the back, possibly because the adults usually sat in the front. I knew their tricks. "I'm going to sit among the restless."

Jaxson smiled. "I will, too."

"I'm staying up front," Rihanna said. "I can get some good shots from here."

"Sounds good." The Hamilton Cemetery was only about two miles from town, so it wouldn't be a long drive.

Penny walked up and down the aisle counting heads. She then held up a thumb to the driver who closed the bus door. As soon as Penny was seated, we took off.

The fairly clear, inky black sky lived up to the forecast. We were lucky in that the moon was almost full, meaning there would be more light in which to see. Should I need it, I had my trusty flashlight. I thought it would be fun to read some of the inscriptions on the gravestones.

Once we arrived, Penny got off first, and one of the two other parents told everyone to gather by Mrs. Carsted for their assignment. Penny hadn't told me what they had planned, but maybe just being in a quiet cemetery at night would be scary enough.

When everyone assembled, Penny separated the students into four groups. She took one group, each of the two moms took a group, and we were given our own group of four. And by we, I meant Jaxson and me since Rihanna wanted to do her photo thing.

"Keep your phone on, okay? We leave in an hour." I hadn't meant to sound like her mom. Sheesh. I was nine years older than Rihanna, but I would be a mess if anything happened to my cousin.

Rihanna smiled. "My phone is on. Text me if something scary goes bump in the night, but if not, I'll be back at the bus by nine."

"Have fun."

"I will."

She lifted her tripod and off she went.

Penny handed me a sheet with four names. "These are your little wards for the next hour."

Jaxson aimed the flashlight at the paper, allowing me to call role. "Ready to check out the monuments?" I asked them.

"I want to see a ghost," said the same little boy who thought Jaxson's outfit was lame.

"I don't think they have cell phones, so I can't call them. And I didn't bring any séance candles with me, but they'll show up if they want to."

That wasn't how it usually worked, but they wouldn't know that. I was just thankful that my grandmother didn't decide to flash the diamond in my magical pink pendant at that moment. That would freak out the kids, though I doubt any of them would believe me if I told them that it was my dead grandmother reaching out to me.

Penny had provided us with a route to follow so that the groups didn't run into each other. "Can you hold the flashlight so I can see where we are to go?" I asked Jaxson.

"Sure. If we'd had this in advance, I could have planned out an exact route," he said.

"It's Penny," I whispered. Organization wasn't her strong suit. I checked the location of our first stop. "It's this way." I pointed east.

As we headed away from the parking lot, the fog on the ground thickened. "Be careful where you step," I warned the kids.

"What is this stuff?" one little girl asked as she stuck her hand in it. "It looks like snow, but it's not cold."

"It's fog."

"What's fog?" a different little boy asked.

Oh, how I didn't miss teaching middle school. Technically, third grade was elementary school, but kids were kids. "Fog is just a cloud on the ground."

"Cool."

I was glad that went over well. A more technical description wouldn't have worked. We were halfway to our destination when an owl hooted, and two arms wrapped around my legs. "What was that?" the frightened child asked.

"That was a ghost," the little boy who didn't like Jaxson's outfit responded.

"A ghost? Will he hurt us?" The poor child's voice shook.

This was supposed to be a fun outing, not a frightening one. "It was just an owl. They love old cemeteries since it's so peaceful here."

"Really?" The little girl wiped her check with the back of her hand.

"Really."

This chaperoning stuff was harder than I thought, but I was determined to make the best of it. We came to the first tombstone. I had no idea why Penny picked this one to check out, but maybe it was because the stone dated back to 1904. The monument had been made from limestone and had not weathered well.

"I think it says, Daniel and Leticia Donaldson." Some of the engraved letters were impossible to decipher. "They died a long time ago," I announced.

"How did they die?" another child asked.

"The headstone doesn't mention how the person died. On the newer headstones, they often put pictures of the deceased or images of something they loved, like their pets or a hobby that was special to them, but that's all."

"Cool, can we see one of those kinds?" one of the little girls asked.

I checked my paper. "We're supposed to follow a path, but let's see if we can find a newer stone."

One little boy took off. "Hey, come back here," I called out. Darn it.

Jaxson touched my arm. "I'll catch him."

I turned to the others. "Please don't go off like that. Some wild animals might be hiding, and if you run, it might scare them into attacking you."

The moment that comment left my lips, I realized that might have been a dumb thing to say.

"What kind of animals?" one brave little boy asked.

I had no idea. "Snakes, maybe, or an alligator who's lost his way, but if we all stay together, they'll keep away. They don't like crowds."

When no one broke into tears, I figured all was well. Jaxson returned carrying the little boy and then placed him on his feet. "Chris won't be running off again."

I didn't want to know how Jaxson achieved that promise, but I'm glad Chris seemed to be okay with it.

"Let's check out the next tombstone area," I announced with authority.

"I want to see a snake," one of the kids said.

"I want to see the alligator. I've never seen one up close." That came from the little girl who'd cried because of the owl.

Oh, boy. I hadn't meant to open that can of worms. Instead of responding, I showed our destination to Jaxson and then motioned that he lead the way. While the moon was fairly bright for the most part, some dark clouds would occasionally float in front of it, bathing the area in darkness. I clicked on my flashlight and aimed it at the ground. I didn't need a child to trip and hit his or her head on a rock. My first aid skills were not current.

The path led us to a wrought iron fenced-in area. Jaxson ran his hand along the top of the railing until he found an opening. After using his flashlight to find the latch, he pulled open the gate.

"Let's see what's in here," Jaxson said.

On the way in, I spotted the sign that indicated this was the location of the Hamilton family graves. "Do you know who is in here?" I asked the four youngsters.

"No," three of them said in unison.

"I know," the sassy boy said.

"Who would that be?"

"A dead person."

The others laughed.

He got me. "You are right. Specifically, Mrs. Hamilton is here. The cemetery is named after her, in fact. When she died a few months ago, she donated a lot of money for its upkeep, so the name was changed to her name." I imagine that was part of the condition of the town getting the money.

"Was she old?" one little girl asked.

"I think so. I really don't know much about her, other than she lived in a really big house on the outskirts of town."

Two of the children looked around. "Where is her grave? Shouldn't it be really big if she was that rich?"

"I imagine it should be."

Jaxson shined his light around the area. Just then, Iggy crawled out of my purse and scurried down my leg. "Iggy," I whispered.

"Who are you talking to? Do you see the ghost of Mrs. Hamilton?" the sassy boy asked.

"No. Iggy is my pet iguana." Oh, boy. He was going to be angry tonight. He highly disliked being called a pet.

"Over here," Iggy called.

I hoped no one could hear him. I wasn't in the mood to explain to a bunch of third graders what it was like to be a real witch—though I'd not met a fake one.

I aimed my light where Iggy's voice was coming from.

He jumped out of the way. "Are you trying to blind me or something?"

"Sorry," I whispered and then moved the light away from

his face.

Thankfully, none of the kids questioned me. Just then Rihanna showed up. "What's with all the flashing lights?"

"We were trying to find out where Mrs. Hamilton's headstone is."

Rihanna stepped next to the area that was devoid of grass. "I was here last week and took a picture of it."

"A picture of what?"

"Of her tombstone. It was a beautiful pink marble monument, colored and engraved." She swung her camera around. "I can show you."

The kids seemed fascinated by this turn of events and gathered around Rihanna as she flipped through the photos. "Here it is."

She held it out to me and Jaxson, and then showed the kids.

The monument had engraved images of red rubies next to a white cat. I would suspect the cat had been her pet.

"Let me see," one of the kids whined.

A bunch of little hands tried to turn the camera in their direction. "That's enough, guys. That's an expensive piece of equipment."

They quieted for a moment. "Where did the stone go?" someone asked.

"Maybe the caretaker noticed a mistake in the engraving and sent it back to the monument maker." I so totally made that up, but it could be true.

Two owls hooted again, and the group huddled closer. It didn't help that a cool chill washed over us. Could that be Mrs. Hamilton's ghost?

While we hadn't been on the cemetery grounds a full hour, it probably wouldn't hurt to slowly walk back to the bus.

"Who wants to go back?" All but one set of the hands went up. "Okay, but be careful where you step. The fog is covering a lot of stuff. I don't want anyone to trip or get lost. That's when the ghosts show up." Lies, lies, and more lies.

We were halfway back to the bus when someone in a white sheet jumped out from behind a tree. "Boo!"

I almost laughed when no one screamed, but the guy did look pretty corny.

"You aren't a real ghost," one little girl said.

"How do you know?" the fake ghost asked.

"I can't see through you."

Smart little girl. When the man tried to explain that he was a different kind of ghost, I decided not to get in the middle of that debate.

Leaves rustled behind me. Uh-oh. I knew that sound. "Is that you, Iggy?" I whispered.

"Yes. Were you going to leave me back there?"

"Of course not." The truth was that I had been rather preoccupied and had forgotten Iggy wasn't in my purse. Eventually, I would have noticed he wasn't there and would have returned for him.

Iggy ran in front of Jaxson who scooped him up. Since it was cold out, Jaxson placed him under his coat. "You spoil him," I whispered.

"It's easier than listening to him complain that you had abandoned him."

Sheesh. I didn't need both of them harping at me.

"Come on kids. Leave the ghost alone. We need to get back to the bus."

When we reached the yellow school bus, we weren't the first ones to arrive. My little group climbed aboard, chatting about their adventure.

I turned to Rihanna. "Did you get any good shots?"

"I think so. I even snapped some guy skulking about."

"Skulking? As in hiding behind the tombstones?"

"I don't know what he was doing, but he gave me the creeps."

I couldn't wait to see her photos once we returned, but since it was late and Rihanna had work to do, I'd view them tomorrow.

Chapter Three

WHEN IGGY AND I returned to the apartment, I offered to fix him a plate of lettuce to make up for my *faux pas* of calling him my pet. While it wasn't his favorite food, the hibiscus flowers were no longer in bloom.

"Were you really going to leave me?"

"I would have figured out sooner or later that you weren't with me."

"Okay."

I didn't expect that answer. "You're not mad?"

"No. I was testing you. I wanted to see if you were going to be truthful. So where is that lettuce you promised?"

I laughed. I had been conned by the little bugger. "I'll get you some."

I made him a plate and then poured myself a glass of wine. The missing pink tombstone troubled me. I wasn't sure if it was my imagination that someone had stolen it or not. I mean, why would anyone take it? It wasn't as if a person could repurpose a grave stone.

Or could they? I'd heard that a tombstone could be sanded down and reused, but I'd read that was more expensive than buying a new one. Not only that, the dead might not be pleased. Or was my imagination running wild like it often did?

Most likely there had been a mistake in the dates or the stone had chipped. The caretaker or family member might have insisted it be fixed.

I picked up the lettuce for Iggy, along with my glass of wine and carried them into the living room. "Here ya go."

I dropped down onto the sofa.

"You look troubled," Iggy said.

"I am."

"Me, too."

I looked over at him. He was chomping on the lettuce. "Why? Does it bother you that someone's grave marker is missing?"

"I guess. When I die, you'll have a marker for my grave, right?"

My stomach flipped. "Don't talk like that. I can't think of something so terrible."

"Fine. What are you going to do?"

I sipped my wine. "About the missing marker?"

"No, about me dying before you do. Of course, I'm talking about the theft."

Iggy was a hoot. "Tomorrow, I will find out if our sheriff is aware of the situation. Surely, the caretaker would have reported it if it had been stolen. Hopefully, Steve Rocker is on the trail of the missing stone."

"Good plan. Now that you're on the case, I can go to sleep. Can you take my plate away?"

It wasn't like he could carry it into the kitchen, but his attitude was rather arrogant. Maybe he actually was upset. "Sure."

As much as I wanted to hash out what might have happened with Jaxson, I had no facts. In all likelihood, there was a perfectly logical reason why the tombstone was gone.

I finished off my wine and then hopped in the shower. When I was done, I crawled into bed and picked up my e-reader, needing to end my day in a world of fantasy.

As was often the case, I jerked awake when the sun streamed in my window. No surprise, my e-reader was face down on my chest. Thankfully, it was only ten thirty, a very civilized hour. Since I had a goal today—that of finding out about the missing tombstone—I willed myself out of bed.

Once I cleaned up, I stepped into the living room. "Good morning, Iggy."

"You seem awfully cheery this morning. And it's not even noon."

"You're a real comedian. I'm happy, because I have a plan."

Iggy closed his eyes and dropped down. "Have fun."

"Oh, no you don't. You can't spend the day sleeping."

"Why not? The more I sleep, the longer I'll live."

That was still bothering him? "Don't you want to be the first one to cross the monkey bridge?"

He perked up. "It's ready? Are you sure it is?"

"No, but how about we see?"

"Okay."

Sometimes, he made life easy. At other times, not so much. I needed my coffee, but I had the sense that Jaxson and maybe Rihanna would like to have breakfast at the Spellbound Diner in order to pick Dolly Andrew's brain. The owner was the recipient of every piece of gossip that came out of the sheriff's office, thanks to his receptionist, who happened to be the sheriff's grandmother.

Iggy hopped into my purse. I walked to the front of our office in order to check out this new crossing. "Do you want to give it a try?"

Iggy poked his head out. "Yes, but if I do, I'll stay over there and visit Hugo."

"You can cross the street, but how will you get into the Hex and Bones to visit him? It isn't as if you can pull open the door yourself."

He looked up at me as if I were totally clueless. "Duh. I'll ask him to open the door for me."

When they were close to each other, they could mentally communicate—or rather Hugo would telepath the information to Iggy. "Don't you have to speak to Hugo in order for him to understand you?"

He stilled. "Oh, you might be right. How about if you put in a lizard door for me, like my cat door? I know you can't make it too big since the store doesn't want any unwanted visitors, but I don't need a lot of room to get in and out. I'm stealthy."

"I'll think about it." Since Jaxson and I owned the building, I guess we could do what we wanted. However, I would ask Bertha, the store owner of the Hex and Bones, if she minded. I had a feeling she'd be fine with the idea. "You take the bridge, and I'll cross the street so I can open the door for your majesty."

"I'm glad you finally understand my role in your life."

Before I could respond to his sass, he scurried up the palm tree and deftly climbed onto the walkway above the street.

While there were no cars at the moment, I wanted to make sure he was okay. The monkey bridge was rather narrow, and it swung with each step.

"You doing okay?" I called up. Yes, I know, if anyone saw me, they'd think I was crazy, but what else was new?

"I'm good."

He didn't sound good, but I crossed the street and waited for him to make it to the Broomsticks and Gumdrops candy store awning. Jaxson had a trellis installed along the side so Iggy could climb down.

Once he reached the sidewalk, I picked him up. "Let's go see Hugo."

"Can I stay there for as long as I want now that I can get back to the office safely?" Instead of his arrogant attitude, he sounded like a kid at Christmas.

"Sure." We entered the store. I didn't see Andorra, Hugo's host, but her cousin Elizabeth was there.

She looked up from the counter and smiled. "I see Hugo is getting a play date."

"He is." I placed Iggy on the floor and let him do his thing. While I was there, I thought I'd ask if she'd heard about the missing tombstone. Her grandmother often had her finger on the pulse of the town, and maybe the information had trickled down to Elizabeth.

"Jaxson, Rihanna, Iggy, and I chaperoned a third grade trip to the cemetery last night and noticed that Mrs. Hamilton's tombstone was nowhere in sight."

Her eyes widened. "That's terrible. Any idea what happened?"

"No. I was hoping you'd heard something."

"No. Nothing."

"Then I'll check with the sheriff." I had a crazy idea. "A tombstone would be really heavy to move. Could say, Hugo, lift one up using telekinesis?"

She shrugged. "Beats me, but when Andorra or Genevieve return, I'll have one of them ask him."

"Great. Oh, and don't worry about Iggy. When he wants to return to the office or our apartment, he can ask Hugo to open the door for him. If you get the chance, check out the new above-the-road bridge we installed for him."

Elizabeth smiled. "Does he know how spoiled he is?"

"I don't think so. Iggy believes he's entitled to such treatment."

After I said goodbye, I headed down the street to the sheriff's office where Pearl was at the reception desk knitting what looked like a scarf—or maybe it was going to be a sweater.

"To what do we owe the pleasure?" she asked.

I smiled and then explained about my chaperoning duties last night. "I was surprised and disturbed to find Mrs. Hamilton's gravestone missing. Just last week, Rihanna had taken a photo of it. It's a handsome piece of artwork."

She nodded. "The caretaker, Charles Langford—though he goes by Chip—was very upset. After all, the cemetery is named after Mrs. Hamilton."

"I know. When was the stone taken?"

"Maybe three days ago."

How was it that I had not heard about this? Someone was slipping. Was it possible that Pearl didn't think the theft was gossip worthy? "May I speak with Steve if he's in?"

"Sure. Go on back. I'll tell him you're on your way."

I had no idea if he had any leads as to who might have taken the monument, but I wanted his blessing to investigate. I knocked on the door and entered.

"Glinda." Steve leaned back in his chair. "What brings you in this early in the morning?"

Apparently, I had a reputation for sleeping in late. Since I'd heard Pearl mention the theft, he must know about it. "I was at the cemetery last night with some elementary aged students when I noticed Mrs. Hamilton's headstone was gone. Pearl said the caretaker reported it stolen a few days ago."

He flashed a brief smile. "Nothing gets by you, does it?"

"Sure it does. If I hadn't been there last night, I wouldn't have heard about it at all."

His right brow raised. "I guess my grandmother is slipping."

Proof that he was aware Pearl was the gossip leak in town, but I didn't want to address that right now. Instead, I sat down. "What do you know about the tragedy?"

"Like my grandmother said, the caretaker reported it missing three days ago. That's all."

I didn't believe him. "Were there tractor marks on the outside of the fence? It's not like anyone could pick it up and carry it away."

"Are you jonesing for my job?"

A laugh escaped. "Hardly. You are very valuable to Witch's Cove. Beside the fact that I'm not qualified to do your job, it seems boring and tedious. It requires too much paperwork."

"You got that right."

"Back to the business at hand. Did Mr. Langford have any theories?"

"No."

He was no help. "Could one of Mrs. Hamilton's relatives have decided to redo the stone's face and hired someone to remove it without Mr. Langford's knowledge?"

"I didn't ask him that." Steve pulled out his trusty yellow pad and made a note. "Any other suggestions on what might have happened? You don't think magic was involved, do you?"

"I don't know. I asked Elizabeth to ask Andorra to ask Hugo if he was capable of lifting a stone of that size."

Steve's eyes widened. "You think a gargoyle is involved in this?"

"No! I just want to understand what we're up against. In this town, anything is possible."

"You can say that again." He leaned forward on his elbows. "Are you planning to look into this?"

I couldn't quite tell what he wanted me say. I honestly didn't think magic was involved, but I'd said that many times before and had been wrong. "Would you like me to?"

"Touché. If you are looking for my permission, you are welcome to ask around. Sometimes a civilian can learn things that a lawman can't."

Finally! It had only taken me a year to convince him of that fact. "Thanks. Does Mrs. Hamilton have any family?"

"Not in town." He tore off a piece of yellow paper and wrote down a name and a phone number. "This is her daughter. I spoke with Mrs. Hamilton's neighbors, and it is my understanding that there was no love lost between them."

"Do we know why?"

"No, but I can guess it might be why Janette Schmidt, her daughter, was told she wasn't going to receive a dime of Mrs. Hamilton's estate."

I whistled. "That had to be tough. If Mrs. Hamilton donated money to the cemetery, I assume she was well off."

"That would be my guess." He flipped through some additional pages on his yellow pad. "I did a little research and found she donated to our local shelter, the county food bank, and various other charities."

"She had a cat engraved on her tombstone. That would imply she was a cat lover," I said.

"How do you know what was on the tombstone if it's missing?"

I held up a finger and pulled out my phone. I texted Rihanna, asking her to email me the photo of the grave marker. Less than a minute later, the image arrived. "Because Rihanna photographed it last week."

I showed him the picture. "Well, I'll be."

Chapter Four

I HAD NO idea what Steve found so interesting about Mrs. Hamilton's tombstone. "What is it?"

"Helen Hamilton's family, along with her husband's family, owned a ruby mine in Madagascar. It's where we believe their wealth came from." He tapped the photo. "These are images of rubies. They kind of look real, but I think they are just lasered onto the stone."

"The monument maker would know. Have you spoken with him?"

"No, but it's on my list of things to check out."

He'd had three days. What had he been doing in that time? It's possible, Steve hadn't prioritized this as his top case. "Who made the tombstone?"

He smiled. "I haven't gotten that far. Once I learn who made it, I'll speak with him."

"I'll ask my mom. Since Mrs. Hamilton died recently, it's possible the family used my parents' funeral home for the service."

He nodded. "That's great. Promise you'll let me know if you find out anything?"

Now, I was almost insulted. "Don't I always?"

Steve dipped his chin. "You and I both know you've kept

things from me."

I didn't remind him that he often kept things from me. So what, if I wasn't a law enforcement agent and he was? "When it involves magic, I don't always pass it on right away, but I will tell you immediately if I think your knowing won't hurt the progress of the case."

"Ouch." He leaned back in his chair. "How about I be the judge of that?"

He was in a sour mood today. "Fine. By the way, how did Mrs. Hamilton die?"

I'm sure if there was any suspicion of murder, the whole town would have heard about it.

"Old age. Heart, I think."

"Was there an autopsy?" Okay, I had seen enough murders to know that when a person was rich, relatives often liked to hurry along the process.

"No. Mrs. Hamilton had heart issues. Please, Glinda, don't go down that path. And no, I'm not going to ask the daughter if we can exhume the body just so you can test it with your necklace."

That was my magical necklace. "I wasn't going to ask." At least not yet. "And Mr. Hamilton?"

"He died two years ago. I think we can wipe him off the suspect list."

Now the sheriff was just plain mocking me. "Thank you for your time. I will ask my mom about the monument maker."

"I appreciate it."

With that, I left. I glanced at the Hex and Bones and then upward at the monkey bridge, but I didn't see Iggy. That was okay. I was sure he was in good hands.

Since I was in dire need of coffee and food, I headed back to the office in the hopes of convincing Jaxson to join me for some breakfast—or was it lunchtime already? I also wanted to see if Dolly knew anything about Mrs. Hamilton since both had lived in Witch's Cove for a long time.

I traipsed up the stairs and then entered the office. Jaxson spun around in his chair. "I was wondering where you were."

Uh-oh. I guess I forgot to text him my morning plans. "Did you call?"

"Yes."

I pulled out my phone. "Whoops. I put the ringer on silent. Sorry." Maybe that was why my phone didn't ping when Rihanna sent the photo.

"No problem. You had a good morning, I take it?"

I must have looked happy or something. "It was productive, starting with Iggy crossing the street successfully using the bridge." I told him about the issue of him being unable to get into the store. "He suggested a lizard door."

Jaxson smiled. "That sounds like Iggy. Let's sleep on it."

He was the rational one. "Are you up for some food? I'm starving."

"Always. The diner or the Tiki Hut?"

"Let's start at the diner. I want to see if Dolly knows anything about Mrs. Hamilton." I nodded to Rihanna's bedroom. When she sent the photo, I didn't ask where she was. "Is she here?"

"No. She went out for a bit." He pushed back his chair and grabbed his keys and wallet. "Let's go."

No sooner had we sat down at our favorite booth than

Dolly charged over. "Pearl said you're going to work the case of the stolen pink tombstone. Is magic involved?"

I busted out a laugh. News sure traveled fast. "I have no idea. I haven't been on the case long enough to make that determination."

I explained about our chaperoning duties, which was how we learned about the headstone—or lack thereof.

"How can someone steal a monument?" Dolly asked.

"That's what has me intrigued—as does why someone would take it. Did you know Mrs. Hamilton? Did she have any enemies? Or do you think this is some kind of innocent Halloween prank?" I don't know how Dolly would know the answers to all those questions, but the woman had amazing connections.

Dolly motioned for Jaxson to scoot over. "I don't think she had many friends—other than her cat. After her husband died, she totally shut down."

"Poor lady. I can totally understand that."

"How did Mr. and Mrs. Hamilton make their money?" Jaxson asked.

I guess I forgot to tell him what Steve said about the source of the Hamilton fortune.

"From the family ruby mine over in Africa." Dolly held up a finger. "But I heard it ran into trouble a while ago. You should have seen their home after that happened. It became an eyesore. The lawn was overgrown and a shutter or two had come undone. And then there was the tile roof. Don't get me started on that."

I didn't realize it was that bad. I'm surprised no one had brought that up. I'd heard more or less where she lived, but

I'd never visited the place. I had no reason to. "Is it still a mess?"

"No. She and her husband were robbed of a very expensive ruby necklace. The insurance money helped bring the mine back from disaster. In fact, the business flourished after that, as did their home."

I whistled. "Did they catch the thief?"

"Yes, it was Chip Langford."

"What? The same Chip Langford who manages the cemetery?"

"The same. He spent a few years in jail for it."

"Was the necklace recovered?" Jaxson asked.

"Not that I know of. I think Miriam knows more. I'd check with her."

By now, the diner was filling up. "Thanks, we will." We both ordered, and Dolly took off.

"That adds a new twist to this case," Jaxson said.

"I know. Do you think Chip Langford had anything to do with the theft of her tombstone?"

Jaxson shook his head. "Why would he? For starters, it would draw too much attention to him since he has a criminal record. He'll be the first person Steve suspects."

"Once a thief, always a thief?" I raised my brows.

Okay, that wasn't nice. My first case—if you could call it that—was trying to help Drake prove that his brother, aka Jaxson, had been falsely accused of stealing from a liquor store. In the end, the former sheriff confessed that he'd framed Jaxson to save his own son. The worst part was that Jaxson had to spend three years in jail for a crime he didn't commit. Finding a job after that had been next to impossible. That might be why he agreed to work with me at the Pink Iguana Sleuths.

"I have sympathy for the guy, assuming he is innocent," Jaxson said.

"Just because the necklace wasn't found, doesn't mean Chip didn't take it. That being said, we should find out more about him. But first, I promised Steve I'd investigate who made the monument. I'm thinking my mom might know."

Jaxson chuckled. "That was a lot of thoughts coming out in one breath."

"As you can tell, my head is spinning." I snapped my fingers. "We could ask Genevieve or Hugo to spend a few days at the cemetery so they can follow Chip around."

Jaxson's lips pulled back. "What good can come of it? Even if they see the cemetery manager go into a shed and break the headstone into small pieces, no court will take the word of a cloaked gargoyle shifter."

Why did Jaxson always have to be right. "Fine. We'll think of something else."

Dolly returned with our coffees and our meal, and I dug in. As delicious as it was, I couldn't focus on the taste like I usually did. This case had taken over my thoughts. I just hoped that the monument maker could provide us with the one clue that would lead us to the thief. But did the stone mason even know Mrs. Hamilton before she passed other than on a professional level?

I was a little hesitant to visit the cemetery manager after what I'd heard, even though I doubted he'd harm us. For now, I'd keep an open mind.

We finished eating, paid, and then walked down the street

to visit my mom. I would have stopped at the Hex and Bones to pick up Iggy, but he complained that he didn't like being at the mortuary. It smelled bad, he claimed. I think he was still traumatized from when Toto, my mom's Cairn Terrier, scratched him—I'm sure deservedly.

We entered through the front and were greeted by the usual yellow runner. It was my mother's homage to *The Wizard of Oz*, her favorite movie. The funeral home smelled of lilies and other fragrant flowers today, but it wasn't as strong as the last time I was there. While it didn't look like a service was going on, soft music was being piped in over the main speakers.

On my way back to where my mom's office was located, I peeked my head in the main viewing room thinking she could be in there.

"I see her." I nodded to Jaxson that we enter. We were half way to the end when my mom looked up and stopped arranging flowers.

"Glinda, Jaxson, this is a nice surprise." As soon as we neared, she kissed us on the cheek.

"It's not like we never come here, but we're on a mission."

"Do you want to come into the office? We won't be disturbed that way."

No one was around to bother us in the viewing room but why argue? "Sure." Once we were seated in the rather small room, she asked what we needed. "Did you do the service for Helen Hamilton a few months back?"

"I did. Why?"

I told her about the stolen tombstone. "Do you know who had made the headstone?"

"I can't be sure, but only Sharpe's Monuments is still in business. The other stone mason closed shop a year or so ago. Sharpe's, if you recall, is the one located a few miles south of Witch's Cove. I'm surprised you didn't know that."

I hadn't been as involved with the business as I probably should have been. "I haven't kept up."

"Well, if I remember correctly, Mr. Sharpe died recently, around the time Mrs. Hamilton passed. I'm pretty sure he was cremated."

I didn't think that was relevant. "Do you remember anything special about Mrs. Hamilton's service?"

"Just that only a few people showed up. The daughter, whose name escapes me, didn't want a fuss. I don't even recall who went to the gravesite."

"Do you know anything about Chip Langford?" Jaxson asked.

"The manager of the cemetery? Not much other than he is very quiet and rather efficient. I heard he used to be a real estate agent."

"Maybe he couldn't renew his real estate license with a felony conviction. Managing a cemetery might have been the best job he could get. Do you know anything about his arrest?"

"No. All I know is that he's never messed up a funeral, and that's all that matters."

"How long has he been the cemetery manager?" Jaxson asked.

"Oh, my. I can't remember. A few years at least."

I asked a few more questions, but we seemed to have exhausted my mother's knowledge. "Thanks, Mom. We might be back if we have other questions."

"You can stop by any time you want. It doesn't have to be about a case, you know."

I smiled. "I know."

After we hugged goodbye, Jaxson and I left. I turned to him once we were out of the office. "Do you want to try to find this Sharpe's Monument company or see what Miriam knows?"

"I need to stop at the office so I can look up the location of the monument company. As for stopping at the Bubbling Cauldron to see Miriam, I'm a bit filled up at the moment." He patted his stomach.

"You got it."

When we entered our office, Rihanna was there. "Hi, guys. Did you find out anything about the tombstone?"

"Kind of." I motioned she take a seat. I filled her in while Jaxson searched for the location of the tombstone maker. "You can see that we don't have anything substantial."

"Mind if I come with you to visit the monument place?"

"I was hoping you'd ask. Your talents are always welcome." I nodded to her camera. "Did the photos of the skulking man come out?"

She chuckled. "Yes. Turns, out it must have been the parent in the white sheet. I guess he was trying to find a place to hide so he could scare the kids."

"Ah, yes. The ghost who wasn't transparent enough for that young girl."

She smiled. "That was him."

Jaxson pushed back his chair and waved his cell. "I have the address programmed in my phone."

"Where's Iggy?" Rihanna asked.

He often came with us. "He's with Hugo. Iggy used the bridge for the first time, and it was a huge success."

She clapped. "I'm so happy for our little man."

"Me, too." I explained the difficulty of him getting into the Hex and Bones by himself though.

"We can get someone to put in a lizard door," Jaxson said. "If, and when, Bertha decides to close the shop, we'll replace the front door."

I leaned over and kissed his cheek. "Thank you."

"Of course."

The three of us left and piled into Jaxson's truck. The monument place was on the far edge of town since Sharpe's business was housed in a large warehouse.

"Do you think it's open?" I asked.

"It should be, unless they don't work on a Saturday." Jaxson pulled into the parking lot where several cars were lined up in front. "This looks promising."

It didn't mean the owner was there. For a change, I decided to keep that comment to myself. I wasn't sure why I was so contrary today, but I was.

We entered the building that smelled of chalky dust. The thin hallway was lined with offices on both sides. We located the one whose stenciled sign read Daniel Sharpe. We knocked, but no one answered.

"I bet he's on the floor," Rihanna said.

"Makes sense." I had no idea which one he'd be, but someone would be able to tell us who ran the place.

As we stepped into the main area, the noise from the drills, sanders, and other equipment was almost painful to my ears. On one side of the warehouse sat stacks of marble, ranging in color from grays to pink, and machines littered the rest of the space. We must have looked lost because a man about thirty-years-old with light brown hair and a fairly fit body, wearing safety glasses neared.

"Can I help you? If you want to pick out a monument, you'll need to come back on Monday when Beth is here. She can take your order."

It made sense that he'd think we were customers. "No, we're here about Mrs. Hamilton's tombstone. Did your company make one for her?"

"Come into my office. It's a bit loud out here."

No kidding, but why couldn't he have answered our question unless he honestly didn't remember? We followed who I assumed was Daniel Sharpe back to the office area. Sure enough, he entered the door labeled with that name.

Before he sat down, he gathered papers off his desk and stacked them on a file cabinet. "Sorry for the mess. I just took over for my dad, and I'm still trying to get the hang of things around here."

Once he motioned we take a seat, we pulled up three chairs. "I'm sorry about your father."

"Thanks. It was really sudden and very unexpected. I thought I'd have a few more years before I had to take over the business."

He sounded as if making monuments wasn't his passion. "What did you do before this?"

"After I received my degree in art and graphic design, I worked for a marketing firm in North Carolina. Admittedly, that skill has come in handy here since I introduced the laser to the firm, but right now, I'm the only one who knows how to use it."

"Did you hear that Mrs. Hamilton's tombstone is missing?"

He nodded. "Chip stopped in and told me. He was quite upset that it was taken on his watch. In fact, he asked that I make another one."

I wonder who was going to pay for it? Chip Langford? "I see. Do you have any theories as to who would take Mrs. Hamilton's monument?" Jaxson asked.

"I have no idea. When my dad made the tombstone, I was living in Raleigh at the time. After Mrs. Hamilton passed, I had the date of her death added."

That was disappointing, in part because his father had passed so we couldn't ask him. "Did the cemetery manager have any theories?"

Chapter Five

"CHIP? NO. HE was terribly upset that something like this happened at his cemetery, but he didn't point any fingers," Daniel Sharpe said.

"Could he explain how someone managed to move the monument without his notice?" Jaxson asked. "That stone is too heavy to carry to the street."

"You are right about that. My guess is that this person had to have used heavy equipment," Daniel said.

Or else a powerful being helped. And no, I didn't believe it was Hugo or Genevieve, but I was willing to bet that they weren't the only two gargoyle shifters in the universe.

"Wouldn't there be evidence of say a tractor moving over the ground?" I asked.

"I'm not a big equipment guy, but if I recall correctly, we had rain two or three days ago. That might have obliterated the tracks. But check with Chip. He'd know."

"Thanks." I slumped in my seat. This was getting rather complicated. "Would Beth know more?"

"I don't know why she would, but you're welcome to ask her. Like I said, she'll be back to work on Monday."

"One more thing," I said. "I saw a photo of tombstone with what looked like rubies. I'm assuming they were designed with a laser, right? They weren't real were they?"

He chuckled. "Definitely lasered on. If they were real, someone would have pried them out the first day."

"That's what I thought."

The three of us thanked Daniel for his time. As we neared the building's front door, I came to a total stop. "Guys," I whispered. "Look at this."

I pointed to the name on the door. "It says Beth *Langford*."

Rihanna moved closer. "Do you think she is related to Chip Langford?"

"That was my first thought. Let's get out of here. We need answers."

Sure, we could have returned to Daniel's office and asked him if she was related to Chip, but if she was involved in this theft in any way, I didn't want to tip her off.

Once we slid into the car, I twisted around in the back seat to face Rihanna. "Before we get into who Beth Langford is, tell me your impression of Daniel Sharpe."

My cousin inhaled. "He's stressed out big time, which makes it hard to get a good read on him."

"But?" Rihanna could usually sense something.

"If pressed, I would say he told the truth. When you asked about Mrs. Hamilton's tombstone, Mr. Sharpe didn't seem to know much about it."

"That's good to know. Jaxson, can you handle some coffee at the Bubbling Cauldron now?"

"I can." I turned back to Rihanna. "Dolly thought Miriam might know something about Chip Langford. Want to come?"

"Absolutely."

After we parked back at our office, we walked over to the coffee shop, which was across the street. Inside, the place was bustling. That was no surprise since people came from afar to experience a Witch's Cove Halloween. Many parents even bussed in their children because the lawn decorations—and candy—were exceptional.

We snagged a table in the middle of the room since everything else was taken. Hopefully, Miriam could get away for a few minutes to chat.

I leaned back against my seat and closed my eyes for a moment to mentally regroup. As soon as we finished here, I needed to tell Steve the name of the monument maker. And I needed to let him know that Daniel didn't seem to know much, because he was living in North Carolina when his father made the tombstone.

"Glinda?" Jaxson nudged me.

I opened my eyes to find Miriam smiling down at me. "I heard you have a new case." She sounded excited.

"Oh, yes. Kind of. Can you spare five minutes to chat? Dolly thought you might be able to help."

She glanced around. "Sure."

Once Miriam sat down, I asked what she knew about Chip Langford. "We've learned that he manages a cemetery, and that he was accused of stealing Mrs. Hamilton's very expensive ruby necklace, but do you know any details?"

Miriam leaned forward. "Just that he was proven guilty and served time for it, but I was never convinced he did it."

Now she had my interest. "Why is that?"

"Chip Langford had it all—a beautiful wife and daughter,

a lovely home, and a great job in real estate."

"He could have wanted more," Jaxson said.

"True, but how many thieves would work on the weekends to help out Mrs. Hamilton and her husband when they were facing financial ruin only to rob them?" Miriam tucked in her chin.

"I would think it would be a good way to case the place." Being so cynical wasn't a good trait, but it was what I believed.

"Nonsense. It wouldn't take months of doing charity work to find out where Helen kept that ruby necklace of hers. She wore it to almost every big event."

Clearly, Miriam believed Mr. Langford was innocent. "Where is Mr. Langford's wife now?"

"As soon as Chip was accused of the crime and went to jail, she divorced him."

"And the daughter?" Rihanna asked.

We still didn't know if Beth Langford was the daughter, the wife, or someone with the same last name who wasn't related to the cemetery manager at all.

"Beth left town with her mom and moved to Columbia, South Carolina, when Chip was arrested. When he had served his time, Beth came back and got a job at Sharpe's Monuments as their lead salesperson. Jaimi, Chip's ex-wife, is still up there as far as I know."

Most likely the wife wasn't involved in any of this then.

"What kind of man was Daniel Sharpe's dad?" I asked.

"Abe? He was an old-fashioned guy who took his time and made quality tombstones. I've heard Daniel wants to modernize the place, and I'd bet anything that Abe wouldn't be happy if he were still alive." Her pursed lips implied she wasn't a fan of updating things either.

How Daniel planned to run the business didn't seem connected to the theft of the tombstone, however. "Any insight into the son?"

"No. I've not met him." She leaned closer. "The thought of death unsettles me. I keep telling Maude that I plan to go first so she'll have to deal with all the sad and nasty stuff. I refused to pick out my own tombstone. I'll leave that to my sister."

"Many people say the same thing." For now, I think we'd picked her brain enough. "Can I get one of your world famous scones and a coffee with a lot of cream and sugar?"

She pushed back her chair and stood. "You got it. What can I get for you two?"

They both ordered. As soon as she left, I turned to my cohorts. "Thoughts?"

Rihanna shrugged. "I'm not getting any vibe here."

"Jaxson?"

"I have this feeling that something is going on with the cemetery manager's daughter, but I don't know what."

I glanced between the two of them. "Do either of you think a woman could move a large stone?"

Jaxson dipped his head. "That's a bit sexist. There are many women who can drive a tractor, especially if her dad can. But, the better question is do I think she has a motive to take the stone? I don't see it, unless she truly believes that her dad is innocent of the theft, and she wants to get back at the family."

I huffed. "What family? Mrs. Hamilton is dead, as is her

husband. Steve only mentioned an estranged daughter."

"Good point."

A server came over with our drinks and snacks. Even though I'd just eaten lunch, I had no problem inhaling Miriam's delicious coffee and scone.

"What's our next step?" Jaxson asked after he'd barely sipped his drink.

"Steve asked that I stop by his office if I found out who made the monument. I also want to know more about Chip."

"What more do you need to know?" he asked.

I shrugged. "Maybe if Chip has gotten into any trouble since he did time?"

"That makes sense. I know a few ex-cons who were repeat offenders."

I didn't need to get into that discussion. "Do you think we should go to the source and ask Chip his take on what happened?"

"Possibly, but I'm thinking he would have told Steve everything, assuming he's not involved."

I smiled. "What makes you think our sheriff would tell me?"

Jaxson flashed me a grin. "Point taken."

We finished our meal, said goodbye to Miriam, and left. I happened to look over at the monkey bridge and spotted Iggy who seemed frozen on the bridge. I nudged Jaxson. "Iggy is doing something, or rather not doing something."

"Let's check it out."

Since we were on the Hex and Bones side of the street, the three of us walked in that direction. Iggy was mumbling, but I couldn't make out what he was saying. If there hadn't been cars driving underneath, I would have walked into the middle of the street and asked him.

"I'll press the crosswalk button," Rihanna said.

"Good thinking."

Thirty seconds after she told the system that she wanted to cross, the light changed. The three of us hurried to the middle of the road and stopped. We had maybe ten seconds to figure out what was going on.

I looked up. "Iggy, are you okay?"

"No. He did it again."

Since the light was about to turn green, I didn't have time to get into a lengthy discussion. I motioned we finish crossing the street. "Meet us on the other side."

With that, we hurried to the other side and waited for him. The problem was that Iggy wasn't moving.

"What's wrong, buddy?" Jaxson asked.

"There's bird poop on the bridge. I don't want to step in it."

Really? Had I raised a wuss? Okay, I wouldn't want to walk on poop, but come on, Iggy was a lizard. "You can do it, Iggy. I'll wash your feet when we get back to the office."

He looked around and then up to the sky. Poor thing. Too bad there wasn't a lizard therapist who could give him some guidance on how to deal with his nemesis. Though if Iggy had been in Hex and Bones at the time of the desecration, he couldn't be sure that Tippy was the offender.

My familiar gingerly moved to the side and inched his way toward us. Once on the other side, he scurried to the palm tree and raced down it.

Iggy seemed to shiver. "That was disgusting."

I had to work not to laugh. "Should we build seagull portable bathrooms?"

"Yes! That's a great idea."

"But if all seagulls are dumb as you claim, how will they know what the enclosed structure is for?"

"I don't know. They can't read either. Other than keeping rats away, seagulls are fairly useless."

Jaxson picked him up and checked the bottom of his feet. He shook his head to indicate almost nothing was there. "I'll take him up and clean him off if you want to talk to Steve," Jaxson offered.

"Thank you."

I couldn't believe we'd paid to have a monkey bridge put in, and then Iggy might never use it. Let's hope the afternoon showers washed away the bird droppings.

Rihanna went back to the office with Jaxson while I crossed the street once more and headed to the sheriff's office. Pearl wasn't at the front desk, and Nash wasn't around either, so I decided to head on back to Steve's office.

Just as I turned the corner to go there, Pearl came out of his room.

"Oh, my. Hi, Glinda."

"Steve asked me to follow up on a clue."

She smiled. "Go right in."

Steve looked up from his computer. "You were fast."

Did he think I'd take days getting the information on the monument maker? I sat down. "The person who made Mrs. Hamilton's tombstone was Abe Sharpe. He used to own Sharpe's Monuments."

"Used to?"

"He passed away around the same time Mrs. Hamilton did. His son, Daniel Sharpe, has taken over the running of the company. I'll cut to the chase. Do I think that he had anything to do with removing the headstone from the cemetery? No. Why?" I explained Rihanna's reading of him.

Steve pulled out his yellow note pad and jotted down the name. "Did Daniel have any idea who might have taken the stone, or more importantly, how someone could have taken it?"

"No. When I asked about whether there had been any tractor tire marks near the enclosed area, Daniel reminded us that it had rained recently, and that the rain could have washed away any evidence. Not that I know for sure, but I would have thought there would still be some rut marks."

Steve nodded. "Let's pretend that someone used a tractor and picked up the stone. Where would they take it? I have a feeling that somebody would have noticed a tractor driving down the road with a headstone in its claw."

"You're right. Even at two in the morning, there are often people on the street. Are you thinking that points to Chip Langford?"

Steve shrugged. "I'm sure you've found out that he was arrested for theft a few years back."

"Yes. He was convicted of taking a very expensive piece of jewelry that belonged to Mrs. Hamilton. They never recovered the piece, so it's possible he was innocent."

"True."

I gave him Miriam's rundown of the man. "He might have been pretending to be a helpful person in order to steal the necklace, or he could have really been a good person."

50

Steve leaned back in his chair. "I only spoke with Chip when he came in to report the theft. I knew nothing of his history or anything about him at the time."

"I see."

Steve dipped his head. "Glinda. I don't like that look in your eyes. What are you thinking?"

Chapter Six

MOST LIKELY STEVE would think I was crazy, but he should know by now that my ideas were out of the box. "What if we're looking at this all wrong?"

His brows rose. "Meaning?"

"The whole tractor thing doesn't sit well with me, unless Chip Langford moved the stone during the day. In that case, no one would think twice about a cemetery manager doing that—assuming he is in charge of handling the tractor."

"Go on," Steve said.

"I know I'm a witch, and I often think along the lines of the occult, but what if someone with magical powers was able to move the stone using telekinesis." I held up a hand. "I'm not suggesting this person possesses the ability to teleport, but a very powerful witch might be able to lift the stone over the fence and then…"

"And then what?"

What would be the next move? "I don't know. First things first. I might ask Levy and his coven if a person of magic can lift something that heavy."

"What about Hugo or Genevieve?"

Darn. I was hoping he wouldn't go there. "I asked Andorra to ask them." Okay, I asked Elizabeth to ask Andorra to ask

Hugo if he could do that.

"What did she say?"

"I haven't spoken with her yet."

"Call her," he said.

In a hurry much? I pulled out my phone and made the call.

"Hey, Glinda," Andorra said.

"Did Elizabeth ask you whether either Hugo or Genevieve could use telekinesis to move a very heavy monument?"

"She did, and I asked both of our resident gargoyles, but they said they didn't know."

I found that rather strange. "Genevieve never tried to move, say, a gargoyle statue?"

"No. However, Genevieve didn't say it couldn't be done, just that neither she nor Hugo have tried."

I suppose I could suggest they lift a car, but if they dropped it, that would be bad. "Tell them thank you. I'm with the sheriff at the moment."

"I see. Well, good luck."

"Thanks." I disconnected and told him what she said.

"It looks like your magical slant might need some refining."

"I still have Levy and his coven." I pushed back my chair. "I'll let you know what I find out."

He seemed to be fighting a smile. "You do that."

More than ever, I wanted to prove him wrong. On the other hand, if a person of magic had been responsible, it would cast the witch community in a bad light.

As I crossed the street to head back to the office, I called my good friend—at least I thought of him as a good friend—

Levy Poole, who was our resident psychic's grandson.

"Glinda!" He always sounded so surprised when I called, and I don't know why. I've asked for his help with the last few cases.

"Hey, Levy, I have a question for you."

"You know I love Glinda Goodall questions. How can I help?"

I explained about the stolen tombstone. "My question is whether you've heard of anyone having the ability to lift a one or two thousand pound monument using telekinesis?"

He whistled. "I know a lot of powerful people, but you are aware that each witch and warlock has different strengths, right?"

I wondered what mine would be—seeing ghosts? "So, you're saying it's possible?"

"I'm not saying anything just yet. Let me do a bit of investigating, and I'll get back to you."

That's the best I could ask for. "Thanks, Levy. You know I appreciate all you do."

Just as I reached the bottom of our office steps, who should be crawling down the railing but Iggy. "Where are you going, mister?"

"I'm going to do battle with those foul seagulls."

"Do battle? Care to explain?"

"They defaced my walkway, and I'm mad."

I lifted him up. "Come upstairs where we can discuss this."

He wiggled in my grasp. "I need to find Tippy."

This was getting out of hand. "How do you know Tippy dirtied your monkey bridge? Did you see him?"

"No, but if he didn't personally do it, then he probably orchestrated it."

I had no idea what to do with him. Usually, having a distraction helped. I opened the office door. "Jaxson and I are going back to the cemetery to speak with the manager, and I'd really like you to come."

He lifted his head. "Why?"

Good question. "You saw firsthand that the monument was missing. You might be able to smell something that we can't." That was lame.

Iggy looked up at Jaxson, who nodded. "Fine."

Not trusting Iggy to not escape, I placed him in my purse and motioned we leave. "Where's Rihanna?" I asked Jaxson.

"Gavin called and said he wanted to surprise Rihanna, which meant he came back for Halloween."

"How sweet. Did she go over to his mom's place?"

"She did."

That meant it was just the three of us. "Let's go then."

"What did Steve have to say?" Jaxson asked as we went down the staircase to the parking lot.

"Not much. I told him my thoughts on Daniel Sharpe, but Steve didn't say much. I contacted Levy about whether a magical entity could lift a stone."

"Can they?"

"He's looking into it."

We slid into Jaxson's front seat. "Did you tell Steve you plan to speak with Chip Langford?"

"Hmm. I don't recall." The answer was no. "I told him I was aware Chip had been accused of theft."

"And Steve didn't warn you not to speak with him?"

"No. If he is a thief, he isn't necessarily violent."

He nodded. "You have a point."

A few minutes later, we arrived at the cemetery. Without a doubt, it was a lot less spooky than it had been during our Halloween night with the kids. Jaxson pulled up to the front of the building that was less than impressive. It seemed to be a working office and not one that dealt with customers—or rather grieving family members. Very often, cemeteries had a separate area that held the crypts.

"Let's hope Mr. Langford is in the office and not out and about the grounds." Then we might not find him.

We walked up the pathway to the building and knocked on the door that proclaimed to be the manager's office.

"Come in," came a deep voice from within.

We stepped inside. Okay, I don't like to stereotype, but this man was gaunt to the point of resembling a skeleton. How had he ever been a successful real estate agent? Perhaps prison had been terrible for him. Or he was sick.

If I had to guess, he looked on the wrong side of sixty, but his rather scruffy beard could have added to that impression. Usually I had a speech ready, but at the moment I was a bit tongue-tied.

Jaxson held out his hand. "I'm Jaxson Harrison. We're helping the sheriff with the theft of Mrs. Hamilton's tombstone."

"Oh, good. I wasn't even sure he was doing anything. Please have a seat."

I finally found my voice, held out my hand, and introduced myself. "Can you take us through to the moment when you noticed the stone missing and whether you'd seen anyone scoping out the area?"

"I don't know if you've been to the site, but it's more or less in the center of the cemetery. Mrs. Hamilton's parents had purchased three resting spots a long time ago. Both are there, and now, so is Mrs. Hamilton. That was before Helen was married, however. When Peter became ill, she purchased a fourth plot and asked that we fence it in so that no one would disturb it."

That hadn't work out well, had it? "Have you had any trouble before with tombstone thefts?"

"No. Never. The Hamilton's are celebrities of a sort, but I've rarely even seen anyone visit the grave. Not even her daughter comes—or at least not that I know of."

"I thought her daughter lived out of state."

He nodded. "I believe that's correct, but people often travel from afar to visit their loved ones."

That was a sad tale. Iggy slightly peeked out of my purse. "Ask him if he did it."

I didn't need to be distracted by my iguana, so I very gently pressed his jaws together to let him know he needed to keep quiet.

"Did you say something?" Mr. Langford asked.

I stilled and let go of my hold on Iggy. "No."

"Tell him," Iggy said. "Or I will."

Tell him what? I lifted Iggy out of my purse. "That was my pet lizard moving about in my bag."

"Pet lizard? You'll pay for that," my sleek little one said.

That was the second time in two days that I'd called Iggy my pet. I would be owing him some special food for that comment.

"He talks?" the manager said.

Oh, boy. "Only to witches and warlocks."

Mr. Langford crossed his arms and leaned back in his chair. "Fine. So, I'm a warlock, but I don't have a lot of power. It's not like I can teleport and steal jewelry out of a locked safe."

Ouch. Not that I really blamed him for being sensitive. If only he knew how many could do that, he wouldn't have used those talents as an example of impossible ones. "I never accused you of anything."

"You didn't have to. I saw the way you looked at me the moment you walked in here. Everyone does. I might have served time, but I didn't take that old lady's necklace. I liked Mrs. Hamilton—until she accused me of theft, that is."

I wanted to disappear. "I believe you."

Jaxson held up both hands. "Hey man, I've been there, done that. Spent three years locked up for something I didn't do. I was lucky enough to have Glinda on my side. She found out who really robbed the liquor store."

It was as if someone had doused the man with a bucket of remorse. His shoulders sagged. "I'm sorry."

"Hey, I get it," he said.

"We really are just trying to help, Mr. Langford," I said. "This isn't about any necklace. This is about who could have removed a tombstone without anyone seeing them, and secondly, learning why someone would have taken it. Did Mrs. Hamilton have any enemies that you were aware of?"

"Everyone has enemies. She was rich—at least for part of her life she was—and others were not. Though when I first met her, she had already let her staff go, because she and Peter were on hard times. That's why I was helping them out."

"I know I'm grasping at straws, but could any hired help have wanted revenge?"

"By stealing a tombstone? What kind of revenge is that? Key a car, throw trash on a person's lawn, or break a window. That's revenge. But take a grave marker after the person is dead? That's not revenge. That's plain nuts."

I had to agree. "Do you have any theories?"

"I wish I did. Like I told the sheriff, I saw nothing. The cemetery is very large. I can't even be positive exactly when the stone was taken."

"My cousin, who is a photographer, was here taking pictures last week. She has an image of the monument, so it was here then."

Mr. Langford stabbed a hand through his hair. "That's good to know."

"I know that when Mrs. Hamilton passed, she donated a fair amount of money to the cemetery, which is why the name was changed to her family name. Do you know why she chose the Witch's Cove cemetery to be the recipient of such a large amount?" Steve never gave me any details about how much was donated or why, but I bet Pearl would know or could find out.

"She didn't tell me. I always figured it was so that her name would live on in perpetuity."

"That makes sense."

"I heard your daughter, Beth, works at Sharpe's Monuments. How long has she worked there?" I asked.

"Ever since I got out of jail. When I was accused of theft, my wife divorced me and move to South Carolina. Beth followed her there. But when I returned to Witch's Cove, my daughter decided to come back."

That matched what Miriam told us. "I'm guessing you two are close?" I asked in my softest voice. I wanted him to trust me. I might not be an empath, but his pain was rolling off him.

"More or less. I'm not an easy man to be around anymore."

Iggy moved along my leg. "Do you drive a tractor?"

Mr. Langford glanced down at Iggy. "I do. Someone has to dig the holes for the caskets. That's my job."

"Would you know if anyone besides yourself drove it in the last week?" Jaxson asked.

That was a good question.

"I have the only set of keys, which I keep in my desk drawer." He pulled it open and lifted out the set to show us. "The office door and desk drawer are locked when I leave at night, and I've not noticed any break-ins."

If he was out and about the cemetery, it would be easy to sneak in and take the keys.

"Are there other workers who could have come in here and made a duplicate set of the tractor keys?" Jaxson asked.

The manager glanced to the side. I had the sense it wasn't one of evasion, but that he truly was thinking. "I don't think so, but anything's possible. When I took over a few years ago, there was only one set. Mind you I have a spare set at home, but no one would find it. Heck, even I'm not positive where I put it."

I believed him.

Iggy half turned around. "I bet there's more than one

tractor in the world."

"Smarty." Though what he said was correct. I placed Iggy back in my purse, stood, and handed Mr. Langford my card. "Thank you for your time. If you remember anything, let the sheriff or us know."

He studied the card, and a small smile came to his lips. "Cute name."

"Thank you."

With my mind spinning, we left. I looked down at Iggy. "Don't say anything until we get in the car."

"What do you think I'd say?" Iggy asked.

That was the problem, I didn't know, but he had a tendency to speak his mind, and no telling what magical talents Mr. Langford possessed.

Chapter Seven

A S SOON AS we climbed into the truck, I faced Jaxson. "What are you thinking?"

"That we need to hear back from Levy to see if a warlock could lift up the stone. Even if Chip Langford has the magical ability to do so, why would he need to?"

Now Jaxson was confusing me. "What do you mean?"

"Chip Langford runs the cemetery. He can do what he wants. No one would question it if they witnessed him taking a stone from the cemetery. They'd think it had to be cleaned—assuming that kind of thing is done—or it needed to be fixed like you suggested."

"I agree. Besides, he sounded so sincere. I just wish Rihanna had been here."

Iggy poked his head out of my bag. "Did you forget about me?"

"No, of course not, why?"

"I'm good with people."

That was news to me. "Are you saying you can read minds like Rihanna?"

"Not like her, but I can sense if a person is good or not."

"Ah, I see, and what is your take on this man?"

"He needs a shave."

I almost laughed. "I have to agree. Do you think he stole the tombstone?"

"I don't think so, but I can't be sure."

Then he really couldn't add much in the way of a character reference. I twisted toward Jaxson again. "How about I call Mrs. Hamilton's daughter? Though I don't know what she'd tell us. On second thought, she wasn't even in town when the stone was taken."

"That you know of."

I had to think about that. "Okay, suppose she was in Witch's Cove. What would be the purpose of stealing her mother's monument?"

"Ah, that is the crux of this case," Jaxson said.

"Even if the daughter was angry that her mom had given money to some animal shelter instead of her, what would be the purpose of removing the headstone?"

"Exactly."

My cell rang. "Oh, good. It's Levy." I swiped the button. "Hey, there. Can I put you on speaker? I'm with Jaxson."

"And me!"

"And Iggy."

"Sure. I spoke to several of my coven members, and no one could name anyone with the power to elevate a one or two thousand pound stone. That being said, Diego thinks he remembers hearing of a warlock who had the ability, but he can't remember who it was."

"Interesting. Would a spell help a person lift something that heavy?"

"I checked a few books, but I didn't see any reference to that. It doesn't mean one doesn't exist, however. You've seen how many volumes we have in the library."

"I definitely have."

"I'm sorry I wasn't of more help this time, but I will keep looking. I'll let you know if I find anything useful."

He sounded dejected. "That's fine. What you told me was helpful. Thank you, Levy."

"You bet."

I disconnected. "That was kind of a bust, I guess."

"Not totally," Jaxson said. "It just means that no matter our opinion of Chip Langford, his name needs to go on the white board as a possible suspect."

I wasn't really sure how he'd concluded that, but the fact that Chip was a warlock qualified him. "I guess."

Jaxson pulled into the office parking lot when my cell rang again. "Ooh, that was fast. Let's hope Levy remembered something." I lifted up my phone. "Oh, it's Steve."

"Glinda, we have a new development."

That sounded intriguing. "What is it?"

"We found the tombstone."

I wasn't expecting that news. "Wow. That's great. Where was it?"

"At the bottom of the ocean. Dave Sanders was leading a group of scuba divers near the caves when he spotted it."

Being on the ocean floor was the last place I would have thought anyone would find it—or put it. "Is it okay?"

"No, and that's the problem. Can you and Jaxson come to the office?"

"You think magic is involved, don't you?"

"Maybe."

Yippee. "We'll see you in a minute." I swiped off the

phone and then told Jaxson what Steve said. "Is that not bizarre?"

"Very much so. Who has access to a boat that is willing to drive a monument out to sea and then dump it in the water?"

"Someone who might be able to use magic to get the stone from point A to point B."

He nodded and then pushed open the driver's side door. "Let's hear what Steve thinks."

Since I didn't trust Iggy not to go in search of his nemesis, I made sure that my familiar remained where he was—securely in my purse.

When we entered the office, Steve was speaking with his grandmother. He looked up, his brows raised. "That was fast."

"We'd just come from speaking with Chip Langford."

"I see. Let's sit in the conference room. Care for some coffee?"

"Music to my ears."

Steve nodded to Pearl to get us some. Once in the glass-enclosed room, we spread out, allowing me to place Iggy on the table.

"Iggy, nice to see you again," Steve said, even though he couldn't hear the response.

Iggy looked up at me. "Should I bob my head?"

I smiled. "Iggy says, you too."

So what if I did a little paraphrasing.

Steve slid two colored copies toward us. "Dave took these photos with his underwater camera. The water isn't crystal clear, but he said the name on the tombstone was Helen Hamilton's with her correct birth and death dates on it."

I looked at the picture. "It's broken in half, only in a very unique way."

"That's why I thought you might be able to add your input, or maybe Daniel Sharpe can."

The stone was cut in half vertically from top to bottom, not horizontally, which would make more sense. I leaned in closer. "It kind of looks like the stone was two pieces in the first place. If not, why is the cut side shiny?" I asked.

"Precisely. More importantly, you can see a neatly carved, polished cavity in the stone."

"It's like the Egyptian kings," Jaxson said.

Okay, I didn't see the connection. "Because?"

"People back then thought that they could literally take their riches with them. That's why the Egyptian kings, and probably other rich people, were buried with gold and other fortunes."

"Are you saying that Mrs. Hamilton encased a few rubies or something for use after she passed?" Steve asked.

"It's possible," Jaxson said.

Pearl came in and handed us some coffee. "Thank you, Pearl."

She smiled and left.

"Do people of magic—not that I'm claiming Mrs. Hamilton is a witch—believe they can spend what they take with them to wherever they go?" Steve asked and then sipped his drink.

Iggy looked back at me. "Does he really think you'd know?"

"I might," I shot back at him. I returned my attention to Steve. "I haven't heard that they do, but I'm not saying it's impossible."

"Maybe it's just old people who fear death and want their belongings with them to bring them comfort."

Before he could say we were of no use, his cell rang. Steve held up a finger and then answered. "Hey, Dave…Fantastic, where is it now?" He grabbed his pen and scribbled something on his yellow pad. "I'll be there." He then disconnected.

"Was he able to raise the tombstone?" I don't know why I asked, since from what I could tell, Dave had salvaged the piece.

"Dave is bringing it in now. We'll have to take a tender to his boat to see it. Want to come?"

I looked over at Jaxson who nodded.

As we headed out, Steve told Pearl he wouldn't be gone long.

"The four of us can fit in my truck," Jaxson said.

"Great."

We all could have fit in the cruiser too, but staring at that cage between the front and the back would be a bit unsettling.

The trip to the marina was a five-minute drive. Waiting for us on the docks was Dave Sanders.

Everyone shook hands except Iggy since he remained in my purse. He'd never been on a boat before, and I bet he believed he might become sea sick.

"The tender is this way."

We followed Dave and piled into the six-person craft. The sea was thankfully calm, but the wind was a bit chilly. Because, I wasn't dressed for the cool ocean breeze, Jaxson must have noticed the goose bumps on my arms, because he wrapped an arm around my shoulders.

After Dave tied off to his large dive boat, Jaxson climbed

up after Steve and then helped me up. On the main deck sat the two parts of the monument. Out in the open, it was clear that a storage compartment had been made in what was the middle of the monument.

Steve knelt down and ran his hand over the smooth exterior. "You said that Abe Sharpe made this marker?"

"Yes, but like I said, he's dead."

"That's inconvenient. Would his son know anything about it?"

I shook my head. "He wasn't in Witch's Cove at the time, but I'm betting everyone else who works for Sharpe's Monuments was. Daniel said he'd had the date of Helen's death engraved, but I don't think he did the actual carving."

"I see. Unless they are open on Sunday, I'll head on over on Monday and ask around," Steve said.

As would we. "There is no way to tell if there was anything in that secret compartment, is there?"

Steve shook his head. "The water would have washed away any evidence."

"The scuba divers and I looked around the monument, but no one saw any jewelry, gold coins, or anything of value in the nearby sand," Dave said.

Iggy poked his head out of my purse. "Can I see?"

"Sure." Who knows what he might find. I told Steve and Dave what Iggy wanted to do.

My iguana crawled out of my bag and managed to get onto the slippery stone. He stuck his nose into the compartment and sniffed. "It smells."

We all laughed. "It probably smells of seawater, buddy," Jaxson said.

"I can see something wedged in the crack. It's blue."

That was different. I translated what Iggy said to Dave and Steve. "Dave, do you have anything resembling tweezers?"

"I do," Dave said. "They come in handy when the engine has issues."

He went to another part of the boat and returned a minute later. "These good?"

They looked like the kind we had in science class. "Perfect." I handed them to Steve. "Do you want to do the honors?"

"It would be handy to either have good eyes like Iggy's or a magnifying glass." He looked up at Dave. "Got one of those?"

"I'm afraid not."

Steve dropped to his knees and looked inside the inset. Just as I was about to ask Iggy to show Steve where he saw the thread, my familiar guided the sheriff's hand to the location. It took a few tries, but eventually Steve found the thread.

"Well, I'll be. Thank you, Iggy." He placed the piece of evidence in a small golden envelope.

My familiar bobbed his head once, which I hoped Steve took as a you're welcome sign. I shouldn't have been surprised that our sheriff carried a specimen envelope. In his line of work, he probably needed it often.

Steve stood. "Any idea how we can get this hunk of stone back to the shore?"

"I have a crane we can use to swing it onto a truck bed, but I need to wait until tomorrow."

The sheriff turned to Jaxson. "Do you think you could coordinate this with Dave?"

"Sure. Where would you like me to deliver it?"

"Sharpe's Monuments," Steve said.

"It'll have to be Monday then, since as you mentioned, they'll probably be closed on Sunday," Jaxson said.

"Works for me."

Once Dave took us back to the dock, we thanked him. During the trip, I had to ask the question that was burning in my mind. "So, we're thinking that Mrs. Hamilton had Abe Sharpe create a storage shelf inside of her monument so that she could stash some valuables in case she could use the money in the afterlife?" I asked.

"It makes sense," Steve said. "The question is who knew she was doing that?"

"I wonder if her daughter knew?" I asked.

"If I asked her, I highly doubt she'd say she was aware of it," Steve said.

I had to agree with him. "If they weren't close, that might be why Mrs. Hamilton didn't leave Janette any inheritance."

Steve tucked the envelope into his top pocket. "That might be cause for murder—which this was not—but I don't see how this relates to stealing a tombstone."

Didn't he? "Hello? What if Janette found out that what she considered was her inheritance was in some hunk of granite. Heck, I might try to open it up and take what I believed was rightfully mine."

Steve whistled. "I need to be more cynical. I could give the sheriff where Janette and her husband live a call and ask him to secure a search warrant for some rubies or the necklace, but the problem is that the daughter may claim that any jewels found were a gift from her parents."

"That could be an issue," I said.

"How about we eliminate all other suspects before I go that route?"

"Works for me."

When we reached our office, it was getting late, and I was starving. It had been a long day.

Steve pushed open the car door. "Thanks for your help."

I don't think we did much. Oh, wait. Iggy found the thread. "I hope the crime lab can identify the evidence."

"I'm not sure how important it is right now. The thread implies something might have been in there. But we need to find the actual pouch in order to prove it came from inside the monument."

"Gotcha."

"Jaxson, call me when the tombstone has been delivered to Sharpe's Monuments, or if you want any help with it, give me a shout," Steve said.

Jaxson saluted. "Will do."

As soon as Steve headed across the street to his office, I faced Jaxson. "You hungry?"

He tossed me a knowing smile. "Which gossip queen is your pleasure?"

Smarty pants. I was beginning to believe he could read minds.

Chapter Eight

AFTER OUR EXCITING and exhausting day yesterday learning about the sunken treasure, I slept like a log. Being Sunday, many places would be closed, so I thought I'd spend the time with the white board, listing who might have been capable of stealing the monument. The motive for the theft was becoming clearer—the potential acquisition of some jewels or maybe gold.

After I was sufficiently fed and full of coffee from the Tiki Hut Grill, I called Jaxson to tell him I was headed to the office. I had no idea if Rihanna would be there, or if she would be with Gavin all day. If I had to guess, we wouldn't be seeing much of her until after Halloween when Gavin returned to school.

"I'm already at the office," Jaxson said once I asked him where he was.

I didn't know why he wanted to be there, but I was happy he was. I turned to Iggy. "You want to come?"

"Why not? If I get bored, I can—or not."

"You can or cannot, what?"

"I was going to visit Hugo using the monkey bridge, but it hasn't rained yet. I need the water to wash away the bird poop."

I couldn't believe a lizard would be so picky about his hygiene. Then again, Iggy was no ordinary iguana.

I returned to my phone conversation. "Iggy and I will be over shortly. I want to work on my white board."

"It's all set up for you."

"You know me well."

Jaxson chuckled. "See you in a bit."

I had the best fiancé. I picked up Iggy, and instead of having him travel in my purse, I let him ride on my shoulder. I was glad that in our two-minute walk none of the squawking seagulls spotted us.

I went in the front way and found both Jaxson and Rihanna, which was a surprise. "Hey, you two."

I placed Iggy on the floor.

"Here to figure out who stole the tombstone?" Rihanna asked.

"I'm going to try." I looked at the cleaned board. "Someone's been busy."

Rihanna shrugged. "I thought I might as well get it cleaned for our case."

"You did more than clean it. You drew the lines and put in the headings." I set down my purse. "I hope both of you will help."

"I'm afraid I can only stay a few minutes. I'm meeting Gavin at the diner for an early lunch."

"I'll take you for however long I can."

"Great. I'm sorry I missed yesterday. Seems like you all had an adventure."

I smiled. "We did, but I have no doubt there will be others."

"I'm sure."

I thought most of the suspects were known to us but writing them down always helped. "I'll start with the known people of magic—Chip Langford and Beth Langford. I can't assume there aren't others, however."

"I agree," Rihanna said.

"Chip Langford had the means to remove the headstone, but what would be his motive?" I asked.

Rihanna smiled. "Easy. Do you really want to see the headstone of the woman who sent you to jail?"

"Maybe not, but stealing it is almost too obvious since people might draw the same conclusion you did. Personally, I would have used spray paint to deface the front. That's better than removing it all together."

"Glinda Goodall, you'd never do that," he said.

"Not me, but Chip might, assuming he had no idea about the secret compartment."

"Perhaps." Jaxson had a cup of coffee in his hand. He walked over to the sofa to get a better view of the board and sat down. "That hidden space has to be the key to solving this case."

Iggy climbed onto the sofa and perched next to Jaxson. "I found evidence that something was there."

"Yes, you did." I wanted to acknowledge his contribution. "Now what we really need is to learn what was in there."

"Considering there were four shiny sides, the monument was made as two pieces and then glued together," Jaxson said.

"If Mrs. Hamilton went to all that trouble of having a secret compartment, she wouldn't leave it empty," Rihanna said.

"Do you think she hid the stolen necklace—the one that wasn't stolen after all?" Iggy asked.

"That is an excellent question. Rihanna, I know you have to meet Gavin, but Jaxson would you like to do some exploration at the library?"

"For?"

"Someone told us that Mrs. Hamilton wore her necklace to a lot of events. Events in this town are often photographed."

Jaxson smiled. "I see. It's hard to spot the missing necklace if we have no idea what it looks like."

"Exactly. And secondly, could it even fit in the six-inch square by one-inch cavity?"

"That I don't know."

Rihanna sighed. "I wish I could stay and help you figure this out, but I have a date."

I hugged her goodbye. "Say hi to Gavin for me."

"Will do."

As soon as Rihanna took off to have a meal with her boyfriend, I turned to Iggy. "How about if I run you over to Hex and Bones to visit with Hugo while Jaxson and I go to the cold, stuffy library? That is, unless you want to go with us? Or you can stay here."

"I'll stay here."

That wasn't what I expected him to say. "Why? You aren't planning to seek revenge against Tippy, are you?"

"*Moi?* Of course not. That would be dumb."

I didn't believe him. "Why don't you want to visit Hugo?"

"Because you might not be there to take me back when

the store closes."

"We aren't going to be gone that long."

"Ah, duh. It's Halloween. Remember? The store might not be open its usual hours."

When did he become so smart? "Good thinking. Make sure you stay inside then unless it's to visit Aimee." Aimee was my aunt's talking cat who lived across the hall from us. She and Iggy had an on again, off again relationship.

"Okay."

I turned to Jaxson. "Ready?"

"As I'll ever be to look at old pictures of Witch's Cove's gentry at a party. Do you even know what Mrs. Hamilton looked like thirty or forty years ago?"

"No, but I'm sure the photos will have captions."

"Then let's do this."

Now I was worried that the library might close early for Halloween. As soon as we arrived, I checked the sign on the door for their hours and breathed a sigh of relief. We had time before they closed.

My friend Delilah was not working the desk, but I knew where the Witch's Cove reference books were kept. "This way."

Jaxson followed me to an area that housed the microfiche machine, a laptop, a printer, and lots of old books. The problem was that I didn't know where to begin. "Since time is of the essence, maybe I'll ask for help."

"Good thinking."

I didn't know the woman manning the desk, but she seemed excited to help. "You're just looking for a photo of Mrs. Hamilton's necklace?"

"Yes. I was told she wore it to many of the town's events."

"What dates are we talking about?" the librarian asked.

"Anytime in the last twenty years maybe?" Mrs. Hamilton had accused Chip Langford of stealing the piece only a few years ago.

"Let me see."

We watched her scour several old articles and books. She was like the Levy of the library world—fast and highly knowledgeable.

The librarian looked up and smiled. "How's this? Photos back then weren't as clear as they are today."

The picture was a frontal view of Mrs. Hamilton in a long gown wearing a stunning diamond and ruby necklace. "It's amazing. Can you make us a copy of this photo?"

"Of course."

A few minutes later, we were walking out of the library with our answer. "That was easy," I said.

"It was. You know, we haven't discussed tonight's festivities."

He was referring to the trick or treaters. "No one will be allowed to enter the back of the restaurant to go upstairs to my apartment, so I'm thinking we should go to your place where we can hand out candy."

"Sounds good. Did you buy candy?" he asked.

I hissed in a breath. "No. Since Aunt Fern wasn't having a gala this year, Halloween kind of slipped my mind."

"You're a witch. Halloween should be one of the most sacred days."

I laughed. "Hardly, but I do like to celebrate it. Let me stop back at my apartment so I can grab my grim reaper outfit. I'll meet you at the office in a few. Then we can see if there is any candy left in the stores."

"Sounds good."

Jaxson parked in front. While I went one way, he went another. Since I would be hungry at some point tonight, I decided to grab something to-go at the Tiki Hut—something that we could reheat in the microwave.

While I was waiting for the cook to fix the meal for me, I couldn't help but wonder how much Mrs. Hamilton's diamond and ruby necklace was worth. She and her husband must have insured it for a lot of money if the sum helped kick-start their family's mining business in Madagascar.

"Here you go, Glinda. Have fun tonight," the chef said.

Even though I missed working here, I enjoyed being a sleuth more. "Thanks."

I knew of an insurance agent who might have been the one to handle the claim, but I really wasn't sure how knowing the value would help us. Nor did I think she'd tell me its value.

After I gathered my Halloween costume, I rushed back to our office. As I entered, I held up the food bag. "I have dinner."

"Great. All we need is candy."

"I hope you don't mind if I take the white board to your place. We only have two names on it."

"No problem." He lifted it up and headed toward the door.

"Iggy, you're coming with us to hand out candy, right?"

He stared at me. "And watch you two smooch in between doorbell rings. No way."

"Fine. I'll drop you off at the apartment then," I said.

Jaxson touched my arm. "I'll put this in the truck if you want to get Iggy settled."

"Perfect."

I took Iggy back to the apartment. "Our place or Aunt Fern's?"

"Aunt Fern's. At least I can talk to Aimee."

"Good choice." I set him down and let him crawl through the cat door to my aunt's apartment. I'd just seen my aunt at the checkout counter. Hopefully, she was enjoying the costumes and not remembering how someone had driven a metal hook into her boyfriend's heart last year. I shivered at that horrid memory.

Once Iggy was safely inside, I rushed back to the parking lot, ready to buy some candy and figure out who might have stolen the tombstone. Considering the manner in which the granite was broken, that should narrow our field.

Jaxson was waiting in the truck. "Ready to scour the town for candy?" I asked as I slid in.

"I am."

It only took us three stops to buy enough. If not many kids showed up, we'd have to give some of it away. Even I couldn't eat that much.

Once we settled in at Jaxson's place, I put both candy bowls on a small table by the door. I then dragged out the white board and stood in front of it with my dry erase marker in hand. "At first, I wanted to finish listing who might be responsible for the theft, but then I was thinking that it might be more valuable to figure out who was aware of Mrs. Hamilton's belief that you could take your money with you to the afterlife."

"Interesting concept," Jaxson said. "I imagine only those who knew her well would be aware of that desire. The question becomes who would that be?"

"I'm betting Abe Sharpe knew since I'm assuming he put in the secret compartment in the first place. Considering his age, though, was he the one who actually made the cut in the middle of the stone?"

"I don't think he would be that old if his son is maybe thirty-five."

"We should ask Steve. Or Elissa Sanchez would know if she did the autopsy."

"For the sake of argument, we'll assume Abe was only sixty-five years young when he passed. And let's say worker *A* made the cuts in the granite, because Abe asked him to. This guy might not have any idea why he was doing it, since some bosses don't always reveal their motives when asking an employee to do something."

I slumped back against the couch cushion. "You're right. Then who would know about the purpose of the secret storage?"

"If Mrs. Hamilton donated money to the animal shelter, maybe there was someone there who knew her well," he offered.

I wrote animal shelter on the board. "What about her other charities?"

"We need to ask Steve for a complete list of them. I just remember him mentioning the shelter and a food bank," Jaxson said.

"Her lawyer would have a list, too, though I don't know

who that is." Needing Steve to get information slowed things down.

Jaxson's brows rose. "Okay, then what do you say tomorrow after we speak with Beth Langford regarding this hidden chamber, we head over to the animal shelter? We know Mrs. Hamilton donated to that. Someone must have worked with her."

"Let's hope, though I'm not sure she would discuss her beliefs about the afterlife to a worker at the animal shelter. I never met the woman, but for some reason she doesn't strike me as that kind of person. We might need to find out who runs the shelter."

Jaxson nodded. "You might be right."

Before we could finish our white board discussion, the doorbell chimed. I made a beeline to the door, but Jaxson remained on the sofa. "Come on. Bring your scythe," I told him.

"I'll scare them."

"Maybe, but once they see the candy, they'll forget all about the menacing grim reaper."

The bell rang again. I pulled open the door and was greeted by three adorable little girls and two moms who were standing a few feet behind them.

"Trick or treat!" they all shouted.

"Look at you cuties. Who are you all supposed to be?" I could guess what two of the three were dressed as.

"I'm a fairy," the little blonde girl said.

"I'm a nurse," the second one chimed in.

"I'm a teacher," the final little girl responded. That was the one I wasn't able to figure out.

"Here's some candy." I gave them each a big handful.

"Thank you," they said in unison and then trotted off.

I closed the door, turned around, and sighed.

"What's wrong?" Jaxson asked.

"Nothing. This is what life should be like."

He chuckled. "Don't tell me you don't like chasing after the bad guys anymore?"

I wrapped my arms around his neck. "I do, but being normal for a few days is good, too."

"Then how about we put the white board away for now and do what normal engaged people do."

"More kids will be coming, you know. You live in a busy neighborhood."

He laughed. "I was talking about turning on the television."

I punched him. "Smart aleck."

Chapter Nine

O N MONDAY MORNING, Iggy and I met Jaxson at the office since we needed to visit Sharpe's Monuments in order to pick Beth Langford's brain. Unfortunately, Rihanna had left for school already, which was a shame since I was interested to find out how her date had been with Gavin. Not only that, having her around when we spoke with someone new was always helpful.

"Learn anything?" I asked as I nodded at his computer.

"Not really. I looked up Sharpe's Monuments, but all of the comments were very favorable. There was no mention of them making any hidden compartments or doing anything unprofessional. And then you arrived."

I was up earlier than usual. "If they advertised secret cubbyholes, it wouldn't be so secret."

"True."

"Ready to see what a certain salesperson has to say about Mrs. Hamilton's tombstone?"

"You bet."

"Before I forget to ask, did Dave call you about picking up and delivering the tombstone?"

"He did. I'm to meet him at three at the docks. He has another charter to finish before he is able to transfer the stone to the truck. Steve will be there to take some pictures."

"That gives us several hours then."

"Yup." Jaxson nodded to my purse. "Iggy in there?"

He stuck his head out. "I'm not missing this trip."

Jaxson smiled. "Good, because we need you to find out if Beth Langford takes after her dad."

"You want me to sneak up behind her and yell *boo*?"

"That could work, since it's in keeping with the Halloween theme," Jaxson said.

"Okay." Iggy slid back down into my bag.

The trip to the monument company didn't take long. When we arrived, the parking lot contained quite a few cars, though I suspected most of them belonged to the workers. It was good to see a local business succeed.

As soon as I stepped inside, Iggy peeked his head out. "What is that smell?"

"Granite dust. Now shush."

I knocked on Beth's door, hoping we didn't need an appointment.

A second later, the door opened. A tall, thin woman dressed in a professional suit with stylish red hair greeted us. "Hello. Can I help you?"

We weren't met with a blazing salesperson smile, but that was probably because most people who came were there for a somber reason.

"I hope so. We don't need an appointment?"

"No. Come in."

On her desk were samples of stones and several brochures. We sat down, and I placed my purse on the floor next to me to allow Iggy to do his thing. I suspected he'd cloak himself so as not to be noticed when he moved closer to Beth.

When Jaxson remained quiet, I figured he wanted me to start the questioning. "We're working with Sheriff Rocker on the case of the stolen tombstone." I liked the sound of that.

She nodded. "Mrs. Hamilton's. It's so terrible."

"Were you aware that Dave Sanders and his dive crew located it?" Jaxson pitched in.

While I couldn't be positive, she might have flinched. "Where?"

Where most divers go. "Near the caves off the coast."

"In the water?"

Was she trying to stall in order to regain her composure? This was why I needed Rihanna to be here. "Yes. What was strange was that the stone had come apart."

Beth shook her head. "Our monuments would never come apart. There must have been a mistake."

I pulled out the photos. "This picture shows the right name and dates. The strange part was that the monument contained a hidden cavity."

Beth studied the photos, showing no signs of fear—only curiosity. "Abe didn't tell me he was doing this, but we do have eccentric people who hope to take their jewels with them."

Jewels? Why not money? Or maybe a keepsake?

"Did you ever meet Mrs. Hamilton?" Iggy asked.

Beth looked over her shoulder, huffed out a laugh, and then returned her focus to us. Bingo! It might be better if we didn't let on that we knew she had magical powers like her dad.

"You never saw Abe put the jewels in the cavity before he

sealed it up?"

"No, but I'm not often on the floor." Beth swept a hand around the room. "This is my domain. I suggest you check with the workers who cut and polish the tombstones."

She might be telling the truth, but I decided not to mention that Steve planned to do that. "If you had to pick one worker who might have watched Abe put the valuables inside the monument, which worker might that be?"

She tucked in her chin. "Any of them could have seen him do it, but none of them would have stolen the tombstone. I spoke with my dad, who is the manager at the cemetery, and he doesn't know how anyone was even able to move it—unless they'd used a tractor."

Jaxson nodded. "We'd wondered that, too. But why move it at all? How hard would it be to hit the stone at the exact angle to break it in half?" he asked.

"I couldn't say. One would need more strength than I have."

Iggy bumped my leg. "Unless you used magic."

Beth stilled. "Did you say something?"

It was time to call her bluff. I looked down at where I thought he was. "Let me see you," I commanded my stealthy familiar.

Iggy appeared, and I lifted him up. "Meet Iggy, my familiar. If you heard him just now, it means you are also a witch."

"So?"

I had to hand it to her. She acted as if it was no big deal to admit it. After all, we lived in Witch's Cove.

"As a witch, what can you do?" I asked.

"Not much. I don't practice the craft anymore. I haven't

in years."

I wanted to ask her whether she could mentally lift a fifteen hundred pound stone, move it a few miles to the middle of the ocean, and then watch it sink. Somewhere during that amazing feat, she had to break the stone precisely down the middle and steal whatever was inside. I would have to say that scenario seemed totally impossible.

"I see." Even if I asked her about moving the tombstone using some kind of magic, she wouldn't admit it, especially if she had committed a crime. "I'll chat with Mr. Sharpe to see if he can help."

"I hope you find out who did this." She sounded sincere.

"Thanks."

Iggy crawled back into my bag and we left. "Let's follow up with Daniel Sharpe later," I said as I motioned we leave.

Before we reached the truck, Jaxson placed a hand on my arm to stop me. "Why not talk to him or the others now? We're already here."

"No one is going to confess to the fact that they watched Abe stuff something of value into a monument and then tried to retrieve it. Besides, Steve said he'd ask around."

"Gotcha, but we need to be certain that Abe didn't steal the items himself."

"I hadn't thought of that. If that were the case, it would mean Mrs. Hamilton told him to hollow out a space for her necklace or some gems and then gave him the items to put inside before sealing it up. That's very trusting of her."

"Agreed. I didn't know the woman, but I'm thinking she wouldn't do that. She'd want to oversee the whole thing from start to finish."

"Yes, but Mr. Sharpe could have taken the monument apart after she left the building," I said. "His company might have needed the influx of cash, and he thought that no one would question where the money came from."

"I have to say, the factory looks up-to-date."

This had potential. "True. The thief wouldn't have known the cavity was empty when he or she stole the tombstone. Are we thinking this thief was so angry when he found out the jewels were gone that he dumped the monument in the ocean, hoping it would sink to the bottom and never be found?"

Jaxson held open his truck door. "I have no idea about that, but I have to say, you have a vivid imagination. I'm not discounting your theory, but the thread Iggy found kind of tells a different story."

"I forgot about that. Ugh. This case rides on the idea that there was a treasure inside, as evidenced by Iggy's find. The key might be to learn what kind of woman Mrs. Hamilton was. Was she the type to hide jewels or something valuable for use after she died?"

Jaxson started the engine. "I'm not sure how anyone would know. How do you plan to find that out?"

"Gertrude is about Helen Hamilton's age. Maybe they knew each other."

Jaxson smiled. "Then let's go visit Ms. Poole." After we parked by our office, we walked over to the Psychic's Corner and found the lobby empty, which made our chances that Gertrude was free a bit higher.

The receptionist smiled. "Looking for Gertrude, I assume?"

I had been there many, many times, usually to visit her. "Yes. Is she free?"

As always, Sarah checked her computer. "She is. I'll tell her you are on your way."

"Thanks." Though a good psychic should know we wanted to see her. So what if Gertrude said that wasn't her strength?

I knocked on her door and poked my head in. "Can we come in?"

"Of course." She motioned that we take a seat on the sofa. Since Gertrude was about ninety, she always sat on a hard-backed chair. In front of her on the table sat a cup of tea. "I hear you've shown some interest in Helen's missing tombstone," she said before we had a chance to ask her anything.

Even if I questioned her about which gossip queen had imparted the information, she probably wouldn't tell me, or maybe she just knew. "We have, mostly because Iggy noticed it was missing, or maybe it was one of the kids who pointed it out."

"And that diver fellow, what's his name?" she asked.

She knew about that? "Dave Sanders."

"He and his team found it and were able to salvage it, right?"

"Yes." I explained how the stone had been assembled, if that was the right word, to form two pieces that were glued together. "Inside was a hidden chamber."

"I see."

Her lack of surprise implied she knew that already. In fact, she might even know what had been in the secret compartment. "Did you know Mrs. Hamilton?"

"I did. Helen and I didn't hang out, as you young people would say, but as the years went on, our paths crossed often enough."

"Was she the kind of person who believed she could take her money with her after she passed?"

Gertrude's brows rose. "Well, she was a witch, so maybe she was hoping she could."

My pulse jumped. "Helen Hamilton was a witch?"

"Isn't that what I just said?"

"Yes. Sorry." I was aware there were a lot of witches in Witch's Cove, but there seemed to be a lot more of them popping up of late.

Jaxson leaned forward. "What can you tell us about her loss of fortune a few years back?"

Gertrude sipped her tea. "The family business off the coast of Africa experienced a collapsed mine shaft that cost a few lives and forced the company to shut down for a while. I heard that put the entire company on the verge of bankruptcy."

"Until her necklace was stolen, and the Hamilton's were paid for its insured value," I mumbled. Yes, I was guessing about the timing of things, but it made sense.

A small smile lifted her lips. "That is what I heard."

"Do you have any idea how much the necklace was worth?" I crossed my fingers that she knew. This was me just being nosy. I don't think the answer would help us find it—not that we were really looking.

"Rumor has it—and you know about rumors in this town—it was worth millions."

Every muscle in my chest tightened. "Oh, my."

"Indeed. The insurance money allowed Helen and Peter to pay off their own debts and then have enough left over to send back to Madagascar to help reestablish the mine."

"I take it, the revenue started pouring in again?" Jaxson asked.

"Yes."

"I wonder why Mrs. Hamilton felt compelled to stash something in her monument?" I asked.

"We'll never know for sure about her need to keep valuables or a sentimental item with her, but she might have decided that no one should have a portion of her wealth if they didn't deserve it," Gertrude said.

Interesting. "Or is it possible the necklace hadn't been stolen in the first place, and she hid it because she didn't want the authorities to find it? Such an event would besmirch the Hamilton name."

Gertrude tilted her head. "You might be right, though I heard Helen didn't want her daughter to be rich after not having done anything to earn the money. My generation is like that."

"What caused the rift between Mrs. Hamilton and her daughter, Janette?" I asked.

"What usually breaks families apart. Money."

That was a bit vague. "Did Janette ask her mother for too many handouts?"

Gertrude smiled. "Good guess, but no. I need to give you a bit of background."

"Please do."

Chapter Ten

GERTRUDE FINISHED OFF her tea. "Helen was born in Madagascar, as was her husband, Peter. It was inevitable that they'd meet since the families jointly ran the ruby mine. When both sets of parents were getting on in age, they asked Peter to take over, but he turned them down. He suggested a cousin of his who had been working the mines for years to take over. You see Peter and Helen had fallen in love and wanted to move to the United States—specifically to Witch's Cove. Peter worked as a financial consultant here for years, but for the most part, they lived off the proceeds of the mine."

"Until they didn't," I added.

"Yes, until they didn't. Turns out the cousin was not a great businessman, but by then Peter wasn't in the best of health, so he wasn't able to return to Madagascar and turn things around. That's when Janette and Hans Schmidt offered to lend a hand. According to some sources, Hans had the qualifications, but Helen said no to his offer."

"Janette didn't take the rejection well, I assume?"

"No, she did not," Gertrude said.

Iggy crawled out of my purse and climbed up the table. He and Gertrude were good friends.

She smiled. "I was wondering when you'd make an appearance, young man."

"I didn't want to interrupt. The story was really good."

"Thank you, Iggy. That is very kind of you."

"Gertrude," Jaxson said. "Did Janette ever threaten Helen?"

"Threaten? Goodness gracious no. It was nothing like that. Janette was the one who gave her mom the cold shoulder. After that Helen cut her off—as in removed her from her will."

"Ouch," Iggy said. He looked back at me. "You won't do that if I'm too demanding, will you?"

"What could you possibly need money for?"

"You never know. Pay off Tippy to stay away from me, maybe?"

I didn't need to get into that can of worms right now. "We'll discuss it later."

Iggy turned back to Gertrude. "Can we do a séance and ask Mrs. Hamilton what she asked Mr. Sharpe to store in the tombstone? I bet she watched him put the items in there and then seal it up."

Go, Iggy. He had been paying attention.

"We can give it a try," Gertrude said. "I don't have anyone coming in for a bit."

"Great."

"Jaxson, will you set up the table that's in the corner?" Gertrude asked as she used her remote to lower the shades and dim the overhead lights.

"Sure." Together we unfolded the séance table and set it up in no time. After gathering the candles she stored in a cabinet, she sat down, and lit them. By now, Iggy, Jaxson, and

I were old pros at contacting the dead.

We touched our fingertips together—or claws as the case may be—and closed our eyes. Iggy had no problem cheating and looking if he sensed a ghost. He'd then let me know if Helen was there.

"Helen Hamilton, it's Gertrude. I imagine you saw that someone took your tombstone and broke it open to get what was inside. What had you stored in there?"

I liked how she went straight to the heart of the matter. That was smart, since ghosts didn't stay around very long. The candles flickered—or something did. I was highly tempted to open my eyes, but I didn't want to ruin anything. This was Gertrude's show.

The air stilled, and then a faint cool breeze blew past my face. In truth, it could have been the air conditioner, but I wanted to believe Helen was there.

"Gems." The word was faint but clear.

"Do you know who stole your tombstone?" Gertrude asked.

"No."

I wasn't aware that ghosts slept, so I thought she'd have known. Maybe she was off at a party with her husband and wasn't watching the gravesite.

"Can you guess?" Gertrude asked.

The lights on the table flickered and then went out. Oh, darn. Not only was she gone, but Iggy hadn't warned me that she had been there.

Gertrude slid back her hands. "She's gone, I'm afraid. Helen might not have built up enough strength to stay around for long," she announced.

That was consistent with what some previous ghosts had told me. "Or else she honestly didn't know."

"Or maybe she didn't want to tell us," Jaxson suggested.

The overhead lights came back on and the shades on the windows lifted. I loved how Gertrude had embraced technology. She placed the remote on the table.

"At least you know there was something there," our host said.

"True, but we aren't any closer to finding out who took the tombstone, or how they did it." Nor could we be sure old man Sharpe hadn't stolen the gems himself.

After we thanked Gertrude and paid for our consultation, the three of us left. "How about we reconvene at the office?" I suggested.

"I'm afraid I need to be heading to the docks to pick up the tombstone from Dave. Remember?"

"Oh, yeah. I'll touch base with the animal shelter people then while you, Dave, and Steve do your thing."

"Perfect."

I tapped my bag to get Iggy's attention. He poked out his head. "You rang?"

"I did. Would you like to come with me to see the animals?"

"Can they talk?"

"Probably not, but I bet they are cute. You don't have to worry. They'll be in cages so they can't hurt you," I said.

"Okay, but wouldn't it be nice if we could get a cage for Tippy?"

"Then he couldn't clean up the beach, which means you know who would come."

"The rats." Iggy ducked inside my bag.

Jaxson leaned over and kissed my cheek. "See you later."

"Good luck moving that hunk of stone."

He stopped. "Do you think Hugo could help?"

I wasn't sure what he wanted the gargoyle to do. "Help how?"

"I'd love to see him try to move the stone using telekinesis."

I shook my head. "What if he drops it? Steve would not be happy."

"You're probably right. If we run into trouble moving it, I'll see what Steve wants to do."

"Sounds like a plan."

Once back at the office parking lot, Jaxson climbed into his truck and took off while I walked to my car, ready to do a little information gathering at the animal shelter.

The shelter was partway between Witch's Cove and Ocean View, but it didn't take long to get there.

"Why are we going again?" Iggy asked as I pulled into the shelter parking lot.

"To get some gossip about Mrs. Hamilton."

"We know there were jewels in the tombstone. What more do you need to know?"

Since when did he become so negative? "I always learn something interesting when I talk to people."

I shut off the engine and grabbed my purse with Iggy inside. In order to reach the office, I had to walk past the animal cages, and my heart broke at all the sadness. If I didn't have Iggy, I would have taken a few of them home.

Iggy poked his head out. "You aren't thinking of getting a

pet are you?"

"No. I can't trust he wouldn't hurt you."

Iggy jettisoned out of my purse and onto my arm. "Me get hurt? You'd have to worry about him."

What pushed his button? "You've never hurt anything in your life."

"Maybe not, but that doesn't mean I couldn't."

Where had this violent streak come from? Right now, I didn't want to find out. "Let's find the office."

Iggy crawled onto my shoulder, probably to show the sheltered animals that he was free, and they weren't.

"There are cats in here?" he asked.

"Yes, and probably a lot of other animals, too. Why?"

"Just wondering."

I hadn't taken more than five steps, when Iggy tapped my shoulder. "Look, it's a rabbit. It's so cute. Can we get him?"

I stopped to admire the fuzzy animal. "I admit he's adorable, but I don't think my small apartment is equipped to take on a pet." I was careful not to lump Iggy in the pet category.

Not wanting to dwell on what these animals must be going through, I walked to the next cage and stopped. Inside was a gorgeous white cat.

"Keep going," Iggy said.

"I like to admire beauty."

The cat perked up and looked at Iggy. "You can talk?"

I don't know who was more stunned, me or Iggy.

"Yes. Who are you?" Iggy asked in a not so friendly tone.

"I was someone's familiar, but she died."

The pieces kind of fell into place. "You aren't Helen Hamilton's familiar by any chance are you?"

The cat's eyes lit up. "Yes, I was. Please get me out of here. It's horrible. There are real animals in here."

If Iggy had to stay in a shelter, it would kill him. I was sure I could find this cat a real home. "What's your name?"

"Ruby. Not original is it?"

She assumed I knew that the Hamilton family owned a ruby mine.

"It's better than Iggy for iguana," my familiar said.

Ruby opened her mouth and what came out sounded like a laugh. Oh, boy. She seemed to sober. "Can you help me?"

"I'll try."

The cat kind of cried as I walked off. Iggy tapped my face. "What are you going to do?"

"Save her. What else can I do? I can't leave her here."

Iggy turned around, crawled down my arm, and slipped into my bag. I guess he didn't want to listen to me negotiating for Ruby's release. There were plenty of witches in town who would love to have a cat. My aunt, for instance, might want someone to keep Aimee company.

I had come to find out about Mrs. Hamilton, but who better than her familiar to give us the scoop. I hated to think what Iggy could tell others about me and my habits after I died.

Inside the office was a young man. He looked up from his computer. "Can I help you?"

He wouldn't be the type of person who would know anything about Mrs. Hamilton. "I hope so. I saw a white cat that I'd like to adopt."

His eyes shone. "Yes, of course. Can you show me which one?"

I didn't realize there were so many white cats, but I escorted him to Ruby's cage. Since there didn't appear to be any name on the door, I didn't want to let it slip that I knew her name. "This one."

"Are you sure? She's not very friendly."

That was probably because Ruby didn't want to be treated as a pet. "I'm sure."

He opened the cage. "Go ahead, little lady."

Ruby looked up at me. "You're sure about this?"

Why wouldn't I be? I nodded as I bent down to pick her up. Ruby purred, probably to impress the worker.

"Looks like a perfect match," he said. "Come back to the office and we'll fill out some paperwork."

"Sure."

Once that nightmare was over, Ruby, Iggy, and I left. While I wasn't able to speak with someone who was aware of Mrs. Hamilton's donation to the center, I got something better—a talking cat.

I placed Iggy in front and Ruby in the back. Knowing my familiar, he wasn't going to accept this new feline easily.

Iggy crawled up the seat and looked over to the back. "Can you do anything magical?" he asked.

I couldn't see Ruby's reaction, but I figured it wasn't a good one. "Iggy, let's let our guest rest for a bit. She's had a big day."

"I hope she doesn't eat flowers," he grumbled.

I didn't like the way he was being so possessive. "Stand down, big boy. No one is taking your place."

Iggy crawled back down. "She better not."

Clearly, I was going to have an uphill battle on my hands.

Rihanna mentioned her lack of having a familiar, so I wondered if she'd want Ruby? The problem was that my cousin spent a lot of time at school and might not be able to care for such a cat. Ruby might be able to talk and all, but it wasn't as if she could feed herself.

Between Aunt Fern, Elizabeth, Penny, and Courtney, someone would want her. Right?

Chapter Eleven

ONCE WE RETURNED to the office, I explained to Ruby that she would be staying with me until we could find a better place for her.

"Why can't I stay here?" she asked as she walked around, sniffing at everything.

Iggy looked at me. "What is she doing?"

I don't know why he asked. His on and off again girl-friend was a cat. "She's getting acquainted with things."

Iggy crawled up my leg and pressed his snout to my ear. "I don't like her here."

I wasn't surprised. "Deal with it for now."

Just then Jaxson came in, his t-shirt stained with some brown sludge. "How did it go?" I asked.

"It was a success in that we were able to move the tomb-stone from the docks to Sharpe's Monuments without incident. I will say that Daniel Sharpe was a bit surprised to get the stone back."

"I imagine he was. Did he show any signs of being scared?"

"Scared? Why would he be?" Jaxson asked.

"While I don't think he personally had anything to do with the theft of the tombstone, maybe he knows who did.

Seeing the stone might create a problem for him."

"I don't think that was the case. He seemed quite happy to have it retrieved."

"I wonder why? Does he plan on reusing the stone?"

"I don't know." Our newest arrival pranced up to Jaxson and sniffed. "Phew. You stink. And who are you?"

Jaxson's eyes widened. "I own this place. The better question is who are you?" He glanced over at me.

I figured it would be faster if I explained. "This is Helen Hamilton's familiar. Her name is Ruby. We found her at the shelter."

"Gertrude mentioned Mrs. Hamilton was a witch." He squatted down and held out his hand. Immediately Ruby pressed her nose against his palm. So much for not liking his scent.

I shifted my gaze to Iggy who surely would not appreciate this gesture of affection. "I'm hoping maybe either Elizabeth, Courtney, Penny, or Aunt Fern might like to have her. They never had a familiar." Though my aunt might consider Iggy's girlfriend a good substitute.

Jaxson looked up at me. "Sounds good."

"I'll figure it out soon enough. Tell me about your salvage adventure."

Jaxson stood. "Let me clean up, and then I will give you the lowdown."

"Sure." While he did that, I went in search of something for Ruby to eat. Sadly, I wasn't well versed in the cat world. "Hey, Ruby. Do you want some milk?"

She pranced into the makeshift kitchen that contained very little real food. "I'm lactose intolerant."

I had no idea. "Okay. What is your favorite food?"

"Fish and chicken. I'm a meat person."

That should be easy. "Let's wait until Jaxson is finished cleaning up and telling us about his day. Then I'll get some meat for you to eat."

"Thank you. What does your lizard eat?"

"Iggy likes flowers and lettuce. He doesn't eat meat."

"Good, then we'll get along just fine."

I wasn't sure if not desiring the same food would make things fine, but I'm glad she was amenable to being around him.

When Jaxson came out of the bathroom, his hair was slicked back, and he'd changed into his spare set of clothes that he kept at the office. He looked good.

"I'm grabbing some tea," I said. "Want something?"

"Water is good."

With our drinks in hand, I returned to the main room. "Tell me what happened?"

He took the proffered drink and sat on the chair opposite the sofa so we could chat better.

"The salvage process took some muscle, but it went fairly smooth, though I don't think my truck appreciated the extra weight. When we arrived at the monument place, Steve showed Daniel what Dave had recovered."

"Was he surprised at least to see the secret compartment?"

"You could say that, but here's the interesting part. Steve asked him to locate the receipt for the job. At first, it looked like it was an ordinary job with the regular paperwork, but then Daniel found a small piece of paper attached to the back of one of the receipts. It was a hand drawing of the compartment."

"Wow. Was there any mention of jewels being stashed in there?

"As a matter of fact, Abe took a photo—which was in another folder—that showed a small blue velvet bag."

That was surprising. "That sort of implies Abe didn't take anything. If he had, he wouldn't have documented it. At least I don't think he would have."

"I'm guessing not."

Ruby pranced up to us. "Mrs. H liked Abe. She trusted him."

I hadn't expected her to know that, but I'm glad she did. "Did your host say if she put rubies in the sack?" I wanted to confirm that the ghost was telling the truth.

"If she did, she didn't tell me. I mean, it's not like I wanted those stupid stones, and she knew that."

"Did you see them?" Jaxson asked.

"No."

"Thank you, Ruby." I turned back to Jaxson. "I don't suppose Daniel had any idea how the thief was able to take the monument apart, did he?"

Jaxson chugged a good portion of his water. "He said the only way to do it was to use intense heat. On occasion, a piece of granite needs to be attached to the main monument. There have been one or two instances where he had to separate the two afterward."

"Why the need to add an extra piece of stone in the first place?"

"I didn't ask. Maybe a child died, and they want the memory to be close."

Ruby was sitting patiently, probably waiting for me to finish talking so I could find her some food. She lifted her head. "Did you know that Mrs. H was a witch?" she asked.

I thought it obvious she'd have to be if she had a familiar, but I didn't want to come off as being a know-it-all. "I did."

"Did you also know that Mrs. H was pretty powerful?"

"No, I didn't. What could she do?"

"It was really cool," Ruby said. "Normally, I'm pretty careful with my claws, but one time there was a lot of thunder, and I jumped on the sofa and kind of tore a hole in the leather."

I didn't see what that had to do with Mrs. Hamilton's powers. "Was she able to stop the thunder?"

"No! She wasn't some superpower. She could run her hand over torn material and mend it."

"That's a real nice talent to have."

"I know, and once someone dented the side of their car, and she fixed it. Pulled the dent out and everything."

"Impressive. She would have made a mint working at an auto body shop."

"I know."

I wanted to speak with Steve and wondered if I could leave them alone for a bit. I suppose if things got rough, Iggy would just leave.

"Jaxson, do you want to join me at the sheriff's department?"

"He knows everything I know. He was there, remember?"

"Yes, but he doesn't know that Ruby can talk. Nor does he know about the alleged insurance fraud or that the rubies might have been stashed inside."

"Ah, yes. You go ahead. Someone needs to supervise these two."

I smiled. That was probably for the best. "Okay."

I had no idea if Steve would even care that I'd rescued a familiar, but maybe he would like to learn that gems were hidden inside the cavity.

Jennifer Larsen, the second shift receptionist, was attending the desk, since Pearl's shift had ended. "Is Steve free for a moment?"

"He's not here. Can I help you?"

This was a bust. "Sure. Can you tell him that I located Mrs. Hamilton's familiar. She's a white cat named Ruby. She is with me at the moment until I find a forever home for her."

Jennifer pulled out a pad and jotted down the information. "I'll tell him."

"Thanks." I probably should have mentioned the results of the séance to her, but I thought it be better to tell him in person.

Before I returned to the office, I decided to do something I'd been wanting to do for a long time: see if I could perform a spell that would allow Steve to understand familiars. In that way, he would be able to communicate with Iggy, Ruby, and maybe even Aimee. My aunt's cat could talk, but she wasn't a familiar—another long story.

There was no guarantee a spell would work. To be honest, I hadn't thought the one I performed on Jaxson would work either, but it had.

As I headed down the street to the Hex and Bones, the sky looked like an early evening thunderstorm was about to let loose, which would make Iggy happy. Then he could cross the monkey bridge without getting his feet dirty.

I had considered asking Aunt Fern to make a pair of shoes for him, but his claws were long and thin. Not only that, he used his feet to grip things. I kind of doubted he'd be able to climb a tree if he wasn't barefoot. Besides, Iggy would have to rely on me or Jaxson to put them on and take them off, and in truth, I didn't want Iggy to grow up being that dependent.

Inside the store, I spotted Bertha right away. She'd helped me last year with the spell. I waved and went over to her.

"Hey, Glinda. I heard you had a case."

"We do, but I'm at a standstill at the moment. Something else interesting happened though."

Bertha smiled. "Oh, yes? What's that?"

I told her our luck in finding Ruby. "She's very pretty and seems very bright. I'd keep her, but Iggy doesn't want her around. You know him. He needs to be the center of attention."

Bertha nodded. "My mother warned me about such a thing. It was why I never wanted a familiar."

I guess that leaves her out of the running. "Do you think Elizabeth might want her, assuming she likes Ruby?"

"She's not here, but I will ask her when she comes in."

I looked around. "Is the rest of the gang in back?"

"No. Andorra is running an errand for me. As for Genevieve and Hugo, they are off doing something." She checked her watch. "They've been gone for quite a while."

"I'm sure they are having fun wherever they are."

She nodded. "I hope so. Genevieve doesn't always possess common sense."

She was a gargoyle shifter who spent most of her life on

top of a church as a statue, so I could understand that. "How well I know, but I came here to see you."

Her eyes shone. "Ooh. How can I help?"

"I need a spell to enable the sheriff to understand Iggy and Ruby."

"Oh. That's new. Is Steve willing to do this?"

That might be my biggest stumbling block. "I haven't asked him yet, but I want to be ready in case he says yes."

"The last spell worked on Jaxson, but you two were emotionally close. That might have been the key ingredient. I can't remember if the spell has worked on anyone else."

"Can we try?" I wasn't one to give up easily.

"Of course. Let me see if I can find the spell. I'll call you when I have everything ready."

I understood that research took time. "Great."

I was halfway across the street when the heavens opened up. Darn it. I ran—well, I moved as fast as I could—and ducked into the Tiki Hut, since I had promised Ruby some food. I didn't imagine the food at the shelter was as good as what she was used to.

Aunt Fern was at the checkout straightening up the paraphernalia in the display case. I tapped on the glass to get her attention. "Hi."

She looked up and smiled. "Well, look who's here—and a bit wet I see. Let me get you a towel."

I was about to say I was okay, but she strode into the kitchen and returned with a hand towel. "Thanks."

Just drying my face and arms did wonders.

"How's the case going?" she asked.

"It's been interesting, but we only have a few suspects.

However, I found Mrs. Hamilton's familiar. It's a white cat named Ruby."

"That's wonderful. How is Iggy handling the new addition?"

I chuckled. "How do you think? I actually stopped over to get some tuna or chicken for her, but in the next day or so, I want to find someone who can take her. It's hard enough dealing with Iggy and Aimee's squabbling, let alone adding Ruby to the mix."

"I understand, but don't look at me. Aimee would not like the competition. She's pretty independent."

"I figured. I was thinking of Elizabeth, Penny, or Courtney might be happy to have her." I see I needed to take my aunt off the list—as well as Bertha, not that she'd been a real contender.

"Those are excellent choices. Go on back, and tell the chef to give you something."

"Thanks, Aunt Fern. You're the best."

Once I told the chef about the stray cat I'd kind of inherited, he fixed me up with some tuna and chopped chicken. I hoped Ruby would be pleased.

With the food in hand, I rushed up to my apartment, changed my shirt, and grabbed an umbrella. Usually, these storms only last a half hour, but there were exceptions.

Let's hope Iggy and Ruby hadn't gotten into an altercation while I was gone. Sometimes Jaxson could become distracted on his computer.

Chapter Twelve

W HEN I ARRIVED with Ruby's meal, I didn't see Iggy. Most likely he was under the sofa, trying to stay away from the newcomer. Ruby, on the other hand, was up on the desk watching Jaxson.

She turned around. "I smell food."

"That's because I have something for you. Come into the kitchen."

Ruby watched me place her meal in a bowl and then attacked it. With her seemingly content, I returned to Jaxson.

"What did Steve say?" he asked.

"He wasn't there, so I left a message." I pulled up a chair and sat down. "I've been thinking, which I know is a dangerous thing, but what do you think about me doing a spell on Steve and maybe Nash, to enable them to hear Iggy, Ruby, and perhaps Aimee?"

His eyebrows rose. "Do you think it will work?"

"I don't know. It worked for you."

"Sure, but I thought since we had a connection it kind of helped."

"That's what Bertha said."

"What do you think Steve will say about having a spell put on him?" Jaxson raised his brows.

That was the problem. "It could go either way, but I won't know until I ask."

"Then go for it."

"I need the ingredients first, and I'm waiting to hear back from Bertha. Once I do, I'll approach Steve."

"Sounds good."

Turns out it wasn't until the next day that I received a call from Bertha. "Hey, Glinda. I think I found what you need," she said.

She wasn't sure? Bertha had been the one to give me the spell that gave Jaxson the power to hear familiars in the first place. "It isn't the same as the one I had before?"

"No. I found that one, but I don't have all of those ingredients anymore. I think this should do just as well."

"Great. I'll be over to pick it up."

Iggy rushed over. "Are you going over to see Hugo?"

"Not Hugo exactly, but I need to pick up something at the Hex and Bones for a spell." I told him that I was hoping we could provide Steve and Nash with the ability to hear him.

"That would be great." Iggy leaned in closer. "What about you know who?"

"You mean Ruby?" He nodded. "I don't think the spell is specific. It might apply to all familiars. Hopefully, it will include Aimee, too."

"She's not technically a familiar," Iggy reminded me.

"I know."

"I want to go with you then."

"Sure." I looked over at Ruby who was coming out of the kitchen licking her lips. "Do you want to go with us?"

"Where?"

I thought she'd have been eavesdropping. I explained about the Hex and Bones and what I needed to pick up there. "There is a wonderful lady there who I think would love to have you."

"Is she a witch?"

"Of course."

"I'm kind of a house cat."

Did that mean she wasn't used to crossing streets, or did she want me to warn Elizabeth about the type of cat she'd be getting? "If you're worried about going outside, don't worry. I can carry you. Iggy can use the monkey bridge."

"Will Jaxson come with us?"

Oh, boy. Someone had a crush. And here I thought most cats ignored people. I looked over at him. "You game?"

"Sure."

The moment Jaxson lifted up Miss Pris—my new name for her—Iggy gave me the stink eye. Hadn't he listened when I said I was trying to find her a new home? Whatever. I'm sure in time, he'd get over his snit.

I carried Iggy as far as the monkey bridge. "You want to check it out? I think the rain cleaned it well enough."

"It better have."

Looking more like a squirrel than an iguana, he scurried up the palm tree and was across the street before we were, which I bet gave him great pleasure in being first.

To my delight, when we entered the store, all three women were there. Iggy took off toward the back while we went to the counter. No one was in the shop, so I had no issue if Ruby spoke.

"Ruby, this is Elizabeth, the lady I told you about. This is

Andorra, her cousin, and this lovely lady is their grandmother, Bertha, the shop's owner. Ruby here was Mrs. Hamilton's familiar."

Bertha must have told Elizabeth about the cat since Elizabeth bent over to be eye to eye with her. "Hi, Ruby. Nice to meet you."

Ruby looked up at me as if she didn't know what she was supposed to do. "Say hi back."

"Hi."

Elizabeth straightened. "She's beautiful. Glinda, Memaw said you were looking for a place for her?"

"I am. Iggy is rather territorial."

"I see. If Ruby is willing, I'd love to give it a try."

Ruby looked around. "Can I stay in the store while you're here? I don't like being left alone during the day."

Most likely this place would be far more interesting to investigate than Elizabeth's apartment. Staying alone might not have anything to do with it. Hopefully, Ruby wouldn't mind being with Hugo and Genevieve for hours on end. They could be a little intimidating.

"I don't see why not," Elizabeth said.

Bertha looked over at Jaxson. "Would you both be okay if I have a cat access installed in the door leading to the back then? That way Ruby can go back and forth whenever she wishes." Bertha leaned forward. "I'm thinking that once the witch population finds out about Ruby, our business might pick up."

That sounded like a win-win to me.

"Sure. I can get that done for you," Jaxson said.

"You are the best."

"Speaking of doors, Iggy wants a lizard door installed in the front so he can come in and talk with Hugo. It will be small."

"Sure. It's your building," she said with a smile.

Iggy waddled out. "Why isn't Hugo here?"

I looked to Andorra. "Iggy," she said. "He and Genevieve are together."

"They're on *another* date?" He sounded rather disgusted.

"People go out more than once, you know." Andorra was very patient with Iggy for which I was grateful.

"I get it, but why can't they be together here?"

That was a good question.

"I don't know, but Genevieve has been acting strange lately," Andorra said more to us than to Iggy.

"Strange, how?" Jaxson asked.

"She's been secretive, but when I asked her about it, she didn't say what it was about, and Hugo's lips are sealed."

That secretive part from her didn't surprise me, but the fact Hugo hadn't confided in his host did. "Hugo didn't tell you anything?"

"I'm afraid his loyalty seems to be more toward Genevieve than to me these days. I have the sense they are up to something, but I don't know what."

"If it has anything to do with the case, let us know. I asked Genevieve about her ability to use telekinesis, so she knows what's at stake here."

"I will."

Two customers came in the shop, and Andorra left to take care of them. I turned to Bertha. "Can you show me how to do the spell?"

"Of course." She placed four spell ingredients, some rocks and candles, along with a piece of paper that contained the spell on the counter. "I can lend you a bowl if you'll return it."

"For sure. What else do I need?"

"Nothing."

Bertha explained where to place the rocks, how many candles to light, and how to mix the potion. "But the most important piece is the spell. Say it in an even, melodic tone, and don't stop for anything."

Really? Could she make it any harder? "What if Steve and Nash are interrupted?"

"That would not be good."

I suppose I had nothing to lose. "How much do I owe you?"

She told me the price, and I paid. I turned to Jaxson. "Are we ready to do this?"

He picked up Iggy and then turned to Ruby. "Do you want to stay here? It won't be much fun at the sheriff's office," he said.

"I guess." I had the sense she was a bit disappointed, but that couldn't be helped. Besides, we didn't need her to be a distraction.

After we said goodbye, we walked down the street to the sheriff's office. "I probably should have called to make sure Steve was there."

"If he's not, we'll come back. It's not like we work far away."

"True."

Inside, Pearl was back at the reception desk. "Hello, you

three. What brings you here?"

Pearl would find out sooner or later. "I want to see if Steve would be willing to have a spell put on him to enable him to hear Iggy."

Her eyes and mouth widened. "That would be incredible. If it works, I'd love to be able to converse with your wonderful fellow."

That was sweet of her. "Let's see if I can get it to work on Steve first. Is he here though?"

"Yes. He's with Nash but go on back."

We walked to his office, knocked, and then peeked in. Steve looked up and smiled. "How's the talking cat?"

"She's fine." I stepped into his office. "I think Elizabeth Murdoch will be keeping her."

"That's good news. So, how can I help you?"

While he didn't tell us to, we pulled out a chair and sat down. Since I was in here so often, I should have a chair with my name on it.

Nash pushed back his seat. "If you'll excuse me."

"No, I'd like you to stay." Being a werewolf, he might have a better chance of hearing Iggy than a plain human.

"You sound serious, Glinda. What's up?" Steve asked.

"I don't know if this will work, but I'd like to try a spell on both of you."

Steve held up a hand. "Whoa. Just stop. I know your spells work, so I will take this seriously. What does this spell do exactly?"

I had been just about to tell him. Impatient much? "It's goal is to make our working relationship a lot easier by giving you both the ability to communicate with Iggy, like Jaxson can."

Steve glanced over at Nash, who sat up straighter. "What do we need to do?" Nash asked.

I was going to make up something wild, but I didn't want him to throw me out before I could say I was kidding, so I went through the exact steps instead. "I've not tried this particular spell before, but I'd like to see if it works. You two just have to sit there."

Jaxson placed a hand on my arm. "I think I'll wait in the other room. I don't want this spell to take away my abilities."

I hadn't thought of that. "Okay. Could you tell Pearl not to disturb us for a few minutes? No calls or anything."

Jaxson looked over at Steve. "You are going to do this, right?"

"Sure. Why not? It can't hurt."

I wanted to rejoice, but I remained professional. "Great."

As soon as Jaxson left, I set up my bowl, rocks, and candles on Steve's desk, hoping I remembered to do everything exactly as Bertha had instructed. When I was nervous, I had a tendency to mess things up.

"Do I need to dim the lights or anything?" Steve asked.

I forgot to ask Bertha, but it would make for a more subdued setting. "Sure."

I lit the candles, and then Steve turned off the overhead lights. It was actually rather nice in there. The problem was my ability to read the spell was reduced because of the dim light, but I was determined to do this.

With the paper in hand, I leaned close to the flame and read the words in a slow, even tone. I personally thought I did a good job, but when I finished, the lights didn't flicker or extinguish like they did in a séance, though Bertha hadn't claimed they would.

"I guess that's it," I announced, trying to sound confident when I was anything but.

Steve stood, walked over to the door, and flicked on the too bright lights. "Now we're almost warlocks?"

I hope he was kidding. I turned to Iggy. "Can you say something?" For the first time in forever, he kept quiet. What was his game? "Fine. Don't talk. I'll ask Elizabeth to return with Ruby."

"No, please."

Gotcha!

Steve's jaw dropped. "You have to be kidding me. It worked?"

My pulse raced. I couldn't believe it. "Apparently, but I can't promise it's permanent. At least you know I'm not making it up when I say Iggy can talk."

"No. I knew you two could communicate."

"Say something again," Nash said.

Iggy faced him. "I like you."

Aw, what a sweet thing to say.

Nash shook his head. "Did he speak?"

"Yes. He said he liked you."

Nash's shoulders sagged. "Why did it work on Steve and not on me?"

If I could answer that, I would be a far better witch. "I have no idea. I'm sorry."

"Yeah, me, too."

Just as I was finished packing up my gear, who should appear out of thin air in the small office but Genevieve and

Hugo.

"This is a surprise," I said. "Genevieve, remember it's not a good idea just to show up," I said.

"Don't worry, we arrived a few seconds ago in our cloaked form. Since I knew everyone, we showed ourselves."

"Okay. Are you here to speak with Steve?"

"And you and Jaxson."

"Let me tell Jaxson to come in. He's probably chatting with Pearl." Or so I assumed.

I opened the door and motioned him inside. He stopped the moment he saw the newcomers.

"How about we all sit in the conference room," Steve said. "There isn't a lot of room here." He turned to Genevieve and Hugo. "Can you two leave the way you arrived and then come back in through the front door this time?"

She smiled. "My pleasure."

With that, she and Hugo disappeared.

Chapter Thirteen

WHILE WE WAITED for Genevieve and Hugo to enter in a more appropriate manner, the five us moved to the conference room. I tried to figure out what would be so important that Genevieve would seek out the sheriff. I could only hope she'd found out who'd stolen the monument.

It wasn't long before our two gargoyle shifters entered through the front. Genevieve chatted with Pearl for a moment before escorting Hugo to the back room.

As if she belonged there, she motioned for Hugo to sit down. Then she joined him. "I know who stole the monument," she announced.

Yes, her attitude was a bit smug, but I couldn't blame her if she really had figured it out. Maybe this was the secret she was keeping from Andorra.

"Who would that be?" Steve asked.

"Grant Stone."

Who? I'd more or less lived in Witch's Cove my whole life, and I didn't know who that was.

Steve jotted down the name. "How do you know he took the headstone?"

She sat up straighter. "Because he told me he did."

This was rather odd. People didn't admit to a crime unless—That's it! "He's a gargoyle, isn't he?"

She did a double take. Nailed it.

"He is."

Nash leaned forward. "Gargoyle or not, why would he confess? And why to you?"

Genevieve leaned back. "It's a long story." She looked over at Hugo and nodded. "Hugo and Andorra were already together when this other gargoyle, Grant Stone, would visit me on top of the church."

Jaxson groaned. "Really? Grant Stone. Not very original, is it?"

She smiled. "No, and he named himself if you can believe it. I think it was a bad choice, but it is what it is. Anyway, after living the double life as a gargoyle and a human, he decided that being a statue was not for him. He claimed being a gargoyle bothered him, despite having the ability to go whenever and wherever he wanted. When he changed into his human form, he vowed to remain that way and to be as human as possible."

I had to butt in here. "Before you finish, did this Grant guy move the tombstone using his powers?"

"You bet he did."

"Sorry, I interrupted. Go on."

"So Grant would visit me, hoping to sway me to run away with him, as you humans would say. I told him no, of course, because I'd already given my heart to Hugo, even though he was with Andorra." Hugo placed a hand on her arm. Aww. That was sweet.

"That's a really nice story, Genevieve, but I'm not understanding this man's connection to the tombstone," Steve said.

She held up a hand. "I'm getting to that. Even though Grant said he was interested in me, his real love in life was money. The problem was that earning money as a human is hard."

I wasn't really following this, but I'd let Steve and Nash lead the discussion.

"Why did he suddenly tell you about stealing the tombstone? And why that tombstone?"

"Like I said, earning money required a lot of work, work he wasn't willing to do. That's why he turned to crime. As far as why did he tell me? I think he wanted to impress me with his new wealth. He pleaded with me one more time to be with him." She shook her head. "And to think I was standing right next to Hugo! Grant must be blind not to see why I'd take Hugo over him."

I don't think she meant she only cared about Hugo's looks. Genevieve truly cared for her friend—or rather her gargoyle mate.

"Didn't he worry you'd turn him in once he confessed?" Nash asked.

Genevieve tilted her head and looked at Steve. I guess she expected him to explain.

"Nash, we can't incarcerate gargoyles. They can come and go as they please."

"Ah, yes, they can teleport and cloak themselves. I forgot."

"Okay, so Hugo and I were on top of the church." She continued as if she hadn't been interrupted. "I won't say what we were doing, but the church is our *special* place. And then along comes Grant. Ugh." She leaned forward. "Hugo calls him Granite Stone." She actually tittered.

Nash didn't even groan. "Did he announce he was a thief?"

"No. Well, kind of. He told me that he'd come into some money. Naturally, I asked him how." She looked over at me. "You said taking money from the bank was wrong, so I was curious how he did it."

"Not only did he move a tombstone, he helped himself to the gems inside, right?" Jaxson asked.

She furrowed her brows. "Almost, but how did you know?"

"A wild guess."

"There were gems inside? Rubies, to be precise?" Steve asked.

"Yes," she said.

"Okay, go on," Steve said.

"Apparently, some former girlfriend of his was in need of getting her hands on Mrs. Hamilton's monument because she was pretty certain what was in there."

"Did he tell you who this woman was?" Steve asked.

"He did. I'm getting to that. As I mentioned, one of Grant's talents is telekinesis."

"Where did he take the tombstone once he left the cemetery?" Steve asked.

"To some stone place where this former girlfriend worked. She said she'd be able to open it up."

We all could guess who Grant was talking about, but I'd let Steve show off.

"It was Beth Langford, wasn't it?" he asked.

Her mouth opened. "You guys are one step ahead of me."

"Not really. Did Grant watch her open the stone?"

"Yes. Apparently, Beth has a few talents of her own. For example, she can heat things up using her hands."

Wow. She was a real witch, with real powers, just like Mrs. Hamilton. If Beth were ever put in jail, though, she could probably melt the bars and escape. But I was getting ahead of myself.

Steve checked his yellow pad. "Was this heat enough to melt the glue that held the two pieces of stone together?"

"He didn't say, but she did get it open, and inside was this bag of rubies."

That corroborated what the ghost of Mrs. Hamilton said. I should have mentioned that to Steve before this, but this was the first I'd seen him. I needed to move her along. "Then what?"

"The deal was that if Grant fenced the gems and got rid of the monument that the two of them would split the money."

"That was very trusting of Beth," I said. "I'd be afraid that Grant would take the gems and never come back."

"I thought the same thing," she said. "Grant didn't give me any details, but maybe she threatened to tell everyone that he was more than just a human."

"I'm not sure anyone would believe her," I said. "But go on."

"Before you do, did Beth Langford think we would be able to figure out who'd stolen the gems if we'd found the tombstone?" Steve asked. "I don't understand why she needed to move it. She could have opened it in the cemetery."

"She might not have wanted anyone to see the secret compartment and know something valuable had been inside," Jaxson said.

"You could be right." Steve turned back to Genevieve. "Sorry. Did he say anything more about where he sold the stones."

"No, but I wouldn't be surprised if he sold some in Paris, London, or some other big city. At least that is what I would have done. The man can teleport, remember?"

I sagged in my chair. There was no way we'd catch the guy. Even if we did, he'd just teleport out of there. Sometimes, gargoyles could be a real danger to us. "Genevieve, I thought you said you didn't know there were other gargoyles here."

"I didn't know any other gargoyles in Witch's Cove. He had a home on the outskirts of town for a while, but eventually he moved someplace out west."

Great. There could be hundreds of them near here then. Who knows how many were good and how many weren't?

"Did Grant tell you anything else that might help us catch Beth?" Steve asked.

"No. After he finished bragging about his exploits, I just wanted him to leave, so I told him to go. I wasn't interested in him, and Hugo here was becoming rather agitated."

Gargoyles could be jealous? Interesting.

"That's good information, Genevieve. Thank you." Steve asked as he looked around. "Any idea where we go from here?"

I snapped my fingers. "Ruby."

"Ruby or rubies?" Steve asked.

"Ruby, Mrs. Hamilton's familiar. I bet she knows a few things."

Steve wagged a finger. "Let's bring her in." He stilled. "I

can understand her, right?"

"You should be able to. Let's see."

I called Elizabeth and asked if she could bring Ruby over to the sheriff's department.

"Why?" she asked.

"We think she might know something about the theft."

"I'll see. Hold on." I could hear some mumbling. "Sure. We'll be right over."

That was easy. I turned to the group. "Ruby will be here shortly."

We didn't have to wait long. The problem was that as soon as Pearl saw Ruby, she had to pet her, and I had a feeling that Ruby was none too happy to be considered anything other than royalty. After all, Mrs. Hamilton had been a wealthy woman.

Steve tapped on the glass and motioned them inside. Elizabeth smiled at Pearl and then headed inside the room. "Sorry about that."

"No problem. Have a seat," Steve said.

"What do you think Ruby knows?" Elizabeth asked.

"Genevieve tells us that another gargoyle was the muscle behind taking Mrs. Hamilton's tombstone, and that he was hired by Beth Langford to do the job." Steve faced Ruby. "Did you know her?"

Ruby looked around. "As a show of hands, how many can hear me?"

I almost cracked up. Who was this animal? Not wanting to be rude, all of us—including Iggy, who lifted his leg—indicated we could hear her. Naturally Nash was the exception.

She looked at Steve. "Do I need to like swear on a bible or something?"

Steve busted out a grin, and trust me, the man rarely lost his composure. "That's only for a court of law, but you are required to tell the truth and the whole truth. I won't be recording this since I assume no one could hear you."

"That's right."

"Then please continue, Ruby."

"Sure. I didn't know Beth Langford well, but I knew her dad. Like I told Glinda, Mrs. H liked Chip Langford. Here's the thing. When things got bad—as in I had to eat generic cat food for a while—Chip started coming by and would do little things for Mrs. H since Mr. H wasn't up to doing much. Bad heart and all. After Chip had been helping out for a few months, I overheard Mr. and Mrs. H talk about insurance money."

"Was this before or after the necklace was stolen?" Steve asked.

"Before."

Steve looked over at Nash. "Are you thinking what I'm thinking?"

"You do know that spell didn't work on me. I have no idea what Ruby is saying."

"I forgot. I'll fill you in later." Steve turned back to the rest of us. "Is it possible that the Hamiltons said the necklace was stolen, but it really hadn't been? And yes, that would be insurance fraud. Since they are dead, there is nothing we can do about that now."

"I'd thought the same thing, but mostly because Chip seems like a sincere guy," I said. "I have no real proof that is he, though."

I swear Steve almost cracked another smile.

"If what Ruby claims is true, it would imply Chip Langford really was innocent. They never found the necklace, you know," Jaxson said.

"I know," Steve admitted.

My head was spinning. For some reason, I didn't think that Ruby had finished her tell-all. "Do you know anything about the stolen necklace? Like was it stolen at all?"

She shook her head, though I wasn't sure if that was a no or just a head shake.

"I didn't hear you, Ruby," Steve said.

She moved to the center of the table, as if she wanted to be the total center of attention. "No, it wasn't. Stolen, that is."

"Tell us what happened," he said.

"It was sad and really wrong—or so Mrs. H told me later on."

Oh, no. She was going to be a story teller like Genevieve by drawing out the details forever. "Why was it sad and wrong?" I asked.

"Why do you think? I liked Mr. Langford. He would bring me the best treats. Mr. and Mrs. H's family business was in some trouble, and they needed money. It was Mr. H who decided they should say the necklace was taken. Only he didn't think the insurance company would believe them. I mean, people in town knew they were in financial trouble."

Dolly seemed to know, so I guess it was well-known. "What did they do with the necklace?" I asked. And yes, I know it was Steve's investigation.

"I don't know. I mean, I wasn't underfoot all the time.

Sometimes I had to eat. They knew I could hear and understand them, but they also knew that I would never give away their secret. Since they are both dead, I figured it won't hurt for the truth to come out."

"Did they decide to frame Mr. Langford?" Steve asked.

"Yes. Mr. H suggested it, but Mr. Langford agreed to do it."

What? No one would do that.

"Why would he say he'd committed a crime when he hadn't?" Steve asked.

She dropped down onto the table, acting as if this discussion was tiring. It wouldn't be if she got to the point right away. "Because Mrs. H promised that if he took the fall for them—whatever that meant—that they'd take care of his daughter if she wanted to finish school or needed money for anything."

"Did she drop out of college?" Chip told us that his wife divorced him, and his daughter moved away with the mom. He never said whether Beth had finished school.

"I think so."

"Ruby," Steve said. "Do you know if Beth Langford ever received this money and if she went back to school?"

"Don't know. Don't care."

That cat had an attitude.

"Okay, let's move on. According to Mrs. Hamilton's will, your host left the house to a real estate company. Do you know why?" he asked.

"No."

"Steve, what was the name of this real estate company?" I asked.

He flipped through his yellow pad. "Oceanside Realty."

I had a real strange feeling. "What firm did Chip Langford work for before his arrest?"

Chapter Fourteen

STEVE LOOKED THROUGH his notes and stilled. "Well, I'll be. It was Oceanside Realty. I don't know why I didn't connect the dots."

"That's no coincidence, is it?" Jaxson asked.

"I suspect not," he said. "I'm wondering if this was Mrs. Hamilton's way of trying to make up for Chip Langford's imprisonment."

"How did that help Chip?" I asked. "I didn't ask him about his employment opportunities as a realtor, but his old firm probably turned him away if he now manages the cemetery. I wouldn't be surprised if Mrs. Hamilton spoke with the mayor and suggested Chip be hired."

"I can ask him, but the mayor might deny it. Doing favors for rich people wouldn't go over well with the constituents."

"True."

"Donating her home to Chip's old real estate firm makes no sense. Any ideas what our next step should be?" Steve asked.

I liked that he also glanced at Ruby. It was cool that he was treating her like a human.

"Maybe Hugo and I can do something," Genevieve said. "We know Beth Langford is guilty—assuming Grant was telling the truth. Hugo can make her talk."

Steve shook his head. "We've been down this road before, Genevieve. Voluntary confessions are one thing, but bending a person's mind is not—or whatever that thing Hugo does is called."

It was so frustrating that Steve insisted we follow the law. "If the gems are worth a lot, why is Beth Langford still working at a monument company?" I asked.

Steve pressed his lips together. "That's a good question."

"Remember, it's only been a few days," Jaxson said. "She might not have had time to spend the money on anything yet."

"Or she is laying low," Steve said. "If she's smart, she won't want to attract any attention for a while."

"Probably true," I said.

"While I'd love to subpoena her bank records, I need a just cause, which is something I don't have." He looked over at Genevieve. "I believe that Grant is guilty, but I don't think saying a teleporting gargoyle shifter confessed to using telekinesis to lift a very heavy monument from a cemetery and effortlessly moved it to a factory, where Ms. Langford proceeded to use her innate abilities to melt the glue between two granite stones would work as proof."

That was one long thought. I needed a moment to process it. "What would each of you do if you came into a lot of money? Maybe it's something Beth would do."

"Go back to school," Jaxson said. "Or maybe she plans to give the money to her dad to help make up for his not-so-great job as a cemetery manger. We shouldn't assume she plans to keep the money for herself."

"That's a thought, but remember Steve can't go digging into Chip's finances either."

"No, I can't. Like I said, I need just cause," Steve said.

We all sat there for a bit. I thought of a few ideas, but there were too many problems with each one. I turned to Genevieve. "I don't suppose Grant would be willing to help us?"

"Help, as in set up Beth?" I shrugged. "Even if I were willing to ask him, I have no idea how to contact him," Genevieve said.

"Do we know who Beth is friends with at least? Maybe they'd know something," Elizabeth suggested.

"I don't know, but we could ask my grandmother to put some feelers out," Steve suggested.

I should be excited at that prospect, but I wasn't. "Even if we locate her best friend, would he or she tell us anything? If they told us something to incriminate Beth, it would mean that person was knowledgeable about a crime and didn't say anything. They'd be arrested."

"Or at least questioned more thoroughly." Steve planted his hands on the desk. "We can speculate all we want, but without more facts, we might be wasting our time. I'd like to do some more research. How about you go home and think about how we can solve this? If Beth is a witch, we might have to resort to magic to solve this case."

I liked the sound of that, but I doubted just a spell would do the trick. We needed a very powerful force, and one that was legal.

Once Steve and Nash stood, we pushed back our chairs.

Elizabeth gathered Ruby and then stroked her head. "You

did great today."

"Thanks, but I wish I knew more."

"You might think of something."

Jaxson picked up Iggy, and we then escorted Genevieve and Hugo outside. We didn't need them teleporting back to the shop. Disappearing and reappearing where someone might see them wouldn't be good.

I hooked my arm in Jaxson's and looked down at Iggy who hadn't said anything the whole time, which I found a bit strange. "You've been quiet."

"I'm thinking."

"I hope it is about the case."

He glanced at me as if I didn't appreciate Detective Iggy Goodall. What had I raised?

AFTER STOPPING OVER at the tea shop, the coffee shop, and the diner to pick everyone's brain, I could barely move from eating and drinking so much.

I had called Andorra and asked if we could reconvene at the Hex and Bones tomorrow to brainstorm how we were going to catch Beth Langford. We decided to meet around one in part to give me time to get up and eat, even though right now food was not on my mind, and secondly, that was when Elizabeth was due in for her shift. Because we wanted her to be with us, Bertha would have to work more hours, but I don't think she'd mind. It was for a good cause.

Andorra said she would set everything up on her end.

I'd already changed into my pajamas and was trying to

read when Iggy came into the bedroom. "I've been thinking some more," he said.

Now he even was sounding like me.

"About what?"

"Ruby."

I didn't think he liked her. "What about her?"

"Does she have any powers like I do?"

Iggy could cloak himself and see ghosts, but I had no idea what Ruby could do. I hope this wasn't about competing with her, though. "I don't know. We'll ask her when we go over tomorrow." When Iggy didn't go back to his stool, I figured he wanted to know more. "What is it?"

"I kind of got a vibe when I was around her."

I almost laughed. I used that word a lot, too. "What kind of vibe?"

"I don't like her. Actually, I can't stand her, but when Ruby is near, my nose itches and my tail twitches."

I had no idea how to respond. "Interesting. We should ask her about it tomorrow." Or should I take Iggy to see a vet?

His chest puffed out. "No! She'll think I like her."

Maybe he did. But what about Aimee? Though I had a feeling Aimee might be happy if Iggy moved on. He had become a bit too obsessed with his seagull problem of late. "Okay. I won't say a word. Now go to sleep. We have a big day tomorrow."

Iggy turned around and left, and I went back to my book, but I wasn't able to focus on the words. I kept going over everything that we'd learned. If Grant was to be believed, Beth had paid him to steal the monument and then fence the jewels. For some reason, it didn't seem right. I couldn't imagine that she'd just hand over rubies worth who knows how much to a former boyfriend no less. Considering the Hamilton's lifestyle, I'd bet the jewels were worth a lot.

I had to find out, or I'd never sleep. I jumped out of bed and went into the kitchen where I'd left my computer.

Iggy followed me in. "You do know I'm trying to sleep? The overhead light bothers me."

I doubted he'd been asleep. It had been less than five minutes since he left my bedroom. "Sorry, but I need to find out how much rubies are worth. I'll just be a sec."

He made some kind of disgruntled sound, turned around, and headed back to the living room. Apparently, the going rate for a ruby didn't interest him.

It took all of a minute to find that some rubies from Africa sold for between eight and fifteen thousand dollars per carat. Considering the size of the hiding place, there could have been twenty stones or more in the bag. That was a nice chunk of change, though the necklace was worth a lot more. The diamonds might have been what jacked up the price.

I closed my laptop and returned to bed, pretty sure I wasn't going to get a good night's sleep. I didn't realize I was wrong until Iggy jumped on my bed.

"Get up," he commanded.

I sat up. "What happened?"

"You're phone has been ringing."

"Who's calling?"

He tilted his head. "Do I look like your secretary?"

I had to laugh at that. Besides, Iggy couldn't answer the phone, though with some ingenuity, I bet he could figure it out. That was assuming the person on the other end could hear him.

I jumped out of bed and retrieved my phone that was on the coffee table. Jaxson had called so I called him back.

"Are you coming in today?" he asked.

I didn't dare look at the time. "Yes. Let me get dressed. Since I need to eat, how about meeting me downstairs in say fifteen minutes?"

He chuckled. "Can do."

I disconnected and rushed to get dressed. It would be good to have a plan going into this afternoon's meeting. Since we'd be heading over to the Hex and Bones in a little bit, I wanted Iggy to come with me.

"Ready?" I asked him.

"I'm going to go over to the Hex and Bones myself. I don't need to stuff my face like someone I know."

"Don't be mean. Besides, how can you get in?"

"Don't know."

"Should I call over there and ask them to look out for you?"

"Yes, thank you." He froze. "Or will *she* be there?"

By *she*, I assumed he meant Ruby. "Most likely she'll always be there from now on. If you want Hugo to remain your good friend, you should talk to him about your concerns."

"Good thinking."

"I'm happy you're willing to climb the bridge yourself, and that you're over your fear of being attacked by the seagulls."

"I'm not afraid. I'm disgusted."

I didn't want to go there. I called Andorra who promised

she'd wait for Iggy to arrive.

"Come on. I'll carry you down the steps your majesty." I lifted him up and set him outside. When I returned inside to the restaurant, to my delight, Jaxson was at the counter chatting with Aunt Fern.

He looked up and smiled. "There she is."

I kissed him briefly and then found a table in Penny's section. My friend spotted me and waved.

"Where's Iggy?" Jaxson asked.

"Iggy went over to visit with Hugo. Maybe between all of them, they'll come up with a plan on how to prove Beth Langford stole the tombstone and the enclosed jewels before we arrive."

Before he could respond, Penny rushed over. "Hey guys. How goes the case?"

I'd only filled her in here and there. "Yesterday, we learned who stole the tombstone." Her eyes widened. "Or at least we think we know that it was Beth Langford."

"Really?"

"How about stopping over tonight for a bit and I can fill you in."

She grinned. "It's a date. Call me with a time."

"Will do."

"Now what can I get you two."

Both of us ordered, and Penny left. I leaned forward. "Iggy said something that has me curious."

"What's that?"

"He wanted to know what kind of abilities Ruby has. There's a possibility she can help us in some way, though I'm not sure how exactly."

"We should ask her."

Jaxson and I came up with a few possibilities for proving Beth was the thief, but none were legal. "We might have to try her in a court of her peers. If she can heat the glue to the point where it melts, no telling what she could do to a metal jail door."

"That is true. She could cause a lot of problems in a regular jail," he said.

The witch and warlock court only cared about the truth. If we obtained evidence by having Hugo or Genevieve spy on her or have Hugo use his gargoyle mind-bending mojo, that might be good enough for a lawyer who specialized in magic. Steve, however, would not be pleased. He never liked having a case left unsolved on his books.

After Penny served us our food, I scarfed mine down. Even though we finished a little before one, I suggested we head on over for our pow wow.

"Let's do it."

Chapter Fifteen

N O SURPRISE, IGGY was in the back of the store when Jaxson and I arrived, but so was Ruby, and to my surprise, they weren't hissing at each other. Maybe it was having Hugo present that allowed the two smaller familiars to get along.

Chairs were in the usual circular fashion. Probably for my sake, Andorra had set up a white board. We believed we knew the guilty party, but it never hurt to jot down ideas for all to see.

We'd all just sat down when Steve came in. I looked over at Andorra, who was sitting to my right.

She leaned over. "I thought he should be here since it's his case."

"I keep forgetting that."

Steve faced us. "Are you all done?"

That broke the ice. Our white board had nothing on it, so he couldn't have believed that. "We were waiting for you." I turned to Ruby. "For the sake of being thorough, do you have any special abilities?"

"You mean can I cloak myself?"

Having the ability to disappear seemed to be a common talent for a familiar—and for gargoyles, too. "Yes. Anything else?"

"I can teleport."

"You can teleport?" The only ones I knew who could do that were in this room.

Ruby swished her tail. "Yes."

One second she was there and the next she wasn't. When she didn't show up for a few seconds, Elizabeth looked a bit nervous.

"Okay, Ruby. You can show yourself," her new host said.

She did, but when she became visible, Ruby had something in her mouth. "What do you have?" I asked.

Ruby jumped down from the chair and pranced over to me. I removed the paper from her mouth. It was a bill—as in our electric bill—to our office. "Where did you get this?"

"Where do you think? I teleported to your office and picked it off the desk. But now I need a nap. Teleporting takes a lot out of me."

Wow. That proved she could teleport. "Okay."

Elizabeth gathered her up, sat down, and placed Ruby on her lap.

Iggy looked up at Hugo as if he wanted some form of assurance that Ruby wouldn't be Hugo's go-to familiar. Hugo shook his head, and Iggy seemed to relax.

"Can you do anything else?" This question came from Steve.

"That's not enough?" Ruby asked.

Steve held up a palm. "Just asking. You are pretty special."

If Ruby could have swooned, she would have. "Mrs. H said I was extra special."

"How so?" Elizabeth asked.

"I don't know if it's true, but she said that I could harness the Earth. I really don't know what that means, but she thought it could come in handy someday."

Harness the Earth? That was special, or at least so I was told. "I'd like to ask Levy to stop over. I know he's wanted to meet Hugo and Genevieve at some point, and I bet he can tell us what harnessing the Earth means. Sound good?"

"Sure," everyone said.

I stepped into the main room and gave Levy a call.

"Glinda, my favorite sleuth. What can I do for you?"

"I have a familiar who says she can harness the Earth, but she's not sure what that means. Would you be able to come over and explain it to us? We're in the middle of a case and need a lot of help."

"Where are you?"

I told him we were across from the Psychics Corner. "We're in the back room."

"Then you're in luck. I'm actually visiting my favorite grandmother now." I could hear mumbling in the background. Most likely Gertrude was telling him she was his only grandmother.

"See you soon." I pumped a fist.

I returned to the room. "Good news. Levy is across the street. He'll be right over."

"Who's Levy?" Ruby asked.

I explained that he was the head of a coven and was highly knowledgeable about all things magic.

"Will he know what I can do?"

"I hope so."

Less than two minutes later, Levy entered the room. I

stood and introduced him to those he didn't know.

Hugo disappeared and then reappeared fifteen seconds later. I turned to Andorra. "What did he do?"

Her head tilted. "Really?" She swiveled around to face Levy. "I want to apologize for my familiar's behavior."

"Was he checking me out?" Levy asked, his lips in a crooked half smile. Apparently, it didn't bother him.

"Yes. He is very protective of me, but he said you were a good guy."

Levy smiled fully. "I'm glad I passed the gargoyle test." He faced me and nodded to Ruby. "I trust this is our Earth cat?"

"Yes, but she doesn't really know what that means," I said.

Levy nodded to Hugo. "Do you want to help me, big guy?"

Genevieve teleported up to Levy. "What do you need him for?"

"Genevieve," Andorra said. "Levy is here to help. He's not here to harm anyone. I promise. You don't need to protect Hugo. He can take care of himself."

"Okay, but I'll need to translate."

"Perfect." Levy turned to Elizabeth. "Can you bring Ruby over here?"

Elizabeth carried her over. "Now what?"

"I want to hold her, but I'd like Hugo's help. Between the two of us, we should be able to sense her powers."

I had the feeling it was more than that, but I kept quiet. I had to admit it looked really strange to see two grown men wrap their hands around the delicate white cat. Levy and

Hugo exchanged glances, almost as if Levy could communicate telepathically with Hugo. Or could he?

After thirty seconds of neither of them saying anything, Levy nodded and then placed Ruby on the floor. "I might be wrong, but I can sense her connection to the Earth. What does that mean? It means she can enhance a familiar's powers or create ones that don't yet exist."

"Really?" Ruby asked.

"Yes. I'm sensing, and Hugo correct me if I'm wrong here, but you and Ruby are power enhancers for some familiars, but perhaps not all of them, right?"

"Hugo said yes," Genevieve responded.

Ruby looked around. "How does it work?"

"Let's say Iggy, for example, could hear well, but when you are near, his hearing intensifies."

"Nope. That's not the case. My hearing is the same whether I'm around her or not." Iggy lifted his head.

Levy motioned that we take a seat. "Like I said, it doesn't work with all familiars. But when it does, it often requires a spell. That spell has to be conducted by the hosts of the familiars."

That was disappointing. "Ruby's host has passed. She's the one whose tombstone was stolen, which is how we ended up here."

He looked over at Elizabeth. "Are you her new host?"

"Yes."

"That might work," he said.

Iggy crawled over to Levy. "Are you saying that Ruby can help me be more special?"

"It's possible."

He looked up at me and then back at Levy. "What will I be able to do?"

"I don't know. We'll have to see," Levy said.

"Oh."

I didn't want Iggy to be too disappointed if this didn't work. "How about if we figure out how to gather proof of Beth Langford's guilt first, and then see if Ruby can help Iggy achieve extra powers that will help us do that?"

Everyone nodded. "Where do we begin?" Steve asked.

I faced him. "What would prove to you that Beth is guilty of stealing the tombstone and the gems?"

"I suppose if we found a blue bag in her possession that contained some rubies, and if the bag matched the thread we found, that would be a good start."

Even though Beth probably would be tried in a court of magic, I didn't want to be limited in my thinking. "You can't get a warrant without proof, right?"

"Correct."

"Grant said he sold the gems," Genevieve said.

"I know, but if Beth was smart, she would have kept a few for herself in case he cheated her," Steve said.

"I know I would have," Genevieve said. "Gargoyles aren't the most trustworthy people."

I'm glad she could be objective.

"If she did keep a few, where do we think she'd hide them?" Jaxson asked. "In her house? In her desk drawer at work? Or in a safe deposit box?"

I slumped in my chair. There seemed to be too many obstacles.

"How about if I, along with Genevieve, Hugo, and maybe

Ruby, cloak ourselves and then teleport to Ms. Langford's house and look around?" Iggy suggested. "Hugo can carry me, since I can't…you know."

"Teleport. Yes, I know. I like the idea, but do you really think she'd keep the jewels out in the open? Can any of you open a locked drawer or safe?" I couldn't help but look over at Levy. He had a friend who could.

"People," Steve said. "Before we go off the rails here, even if you found the jewels, we can't use it against her. They wouldn't be obtained legally."

I thought Jaxson was a spoilsport, but no. Steve was worse.

"Steve," Jaxson said. "If this woman can heat up granite to the point where it melts the glue between the slabs, I don't think you can incarcerate her, even if she signs a confession."

The sheriff's lips pressed together. "You're probably right. What do you propose?"

That was the problem. I didn't know.

"I have an idea," Levy said.

"What is it?" I asked.

"What if you, Elizabeth, Iggy, Ruby, and I take the day to figure out what these two familiars can do. That might help us figure out how to proceed?"

Iggy spun around three times, indicating his excitement. That was not quite what I expected his reaction to be since Ruby was involved. "I'm good with it, but if Ruby can enhance Iggy's abilities, do we have any idea how long a spell like that will last?"

"No. This is new territory for me."

Levy had a great track record, though. "I say, let's give it a try."

After we discussed the plan a bit more, we agreed this might be the best route.

Steve stood. "Glinda, let me know what you plan to do before you do it. Okay? I realize this is Witch's Cove and Beth might not be a suitable candidate for incarceration, but let's try to do this as legally as possible."

"Of course." Or not. Once we had proof, he might not care how we obtained it.

Andorra stood. "I'll let you guys do your thing. I'm going to help Memaw in the store, but if you need me, let me know."

"Thanks for setting up this session."

She smiled. "Sure."

I turned to Levy. "You're up."

"Iggy and Ruby, let's see what you guys can do."

TWO HOURS LATER, my brain was fried. Levy had put those two through their paces, and Elizabeth and I must have done five or six spells. Even though I had no idea what I was doing, I followed Levy's instructions to the letter.

Iggy dropped down on his stomach. "Does Ruby really need to be touching me for me to move through a solid object?"

"In this case, I'm afraid so," Levy said.

"Bummer," Iggy said. "So what's the plan?"

Was he in charge now? Since he had these new powers—at least temporarily—maybe he should be. Steve wasn't here, so we were free to discuss whatever we needed to do.

"Our goal should be to find that blue bag, even if it is empty. Then Steve can match the thread that Iggy found in the tombstone," I suggested to the remaining members of the group.

"I like it. Hugo and I will go with Iggy and Ruby to Beth's house," Genevieve said. "Hugo can be our lookout and stop Beth from coming inside the house should she decide to show up unexpectedly."

Jaxson lifted his hand. "I can keep a watch on Sharpe's Monument and contact Genevieve if I see Beth leave work."

This was sounding good. "How much time do you all need to find some evidence, do you think?"

They all looked at each other. "However long it takes," Genevieve said.

"When will you do this?" I asked.

Genevieve looked over at Jaxson. "What do you think?" she asked.

"I suggest we go tomorrow, as soon as we learn Beth has left for the office," he said. "No telling if the bag or any jewels are in her house, but you need to look. We can't be sure she didn't hand the bag over to Grant, since he needed to sell them."

I groaned. That would be terrible if she had. "Maybe we'll get lucky."

"Iggy, how about I come—or rather teleport—to your apartment tomorrow at ten and we can go from there?" Genevieve asked.

Iggy looked up at me, I guess for permission. "Sounds good, but I'd love to be able to watch," I said.

"Do you want me to clip on one of those camera things like Steve had me wear in the past?"

I really did, but what if Steve told us not to do this little sting operation? "That's okay. You have a cell phone, so take some pictures. Can you do that?"

"I can."

"Great." I turned to Iggy. "Do you want to go back with us to the office, or stay here and plan?"

"I'll stay here."

"I can return him to your office when we're done," Genevieve said.

"Thank you and good luck tomorrow." I just hoped the spell that Elizabeth and I did on Iggy and Ruby lasted that long.

Chapter Sixteen

J AXSON SWIVELED AROUND in his desk chair. He'd returned fifteen minutes earlier from sitting in the parking lot of the monument company for two hours. He left because he said too many people were watching him. "Glinda, can you stop tapping your foot?"

"Sorry. It's just that they've been gone for hours." I felt better about everything last night after Penny and I hashed out the plan. "I'm worried that the spell we did yesterday will wear off when Iggy is in the middle of things."

"If that happens, you and Elizabeth can redo the spell and try again tomorrow."

"I guess so."

"Stop worrying. What can go wrong? They have Genevieve and Hugo."

"Famous last words." I was about to suggest we go to the tea or coffee shop so I could down something sugary when my cell rang. "It's Andorra."

"Yes?"

She chuckled. "You sound stressed."

"You think? Did you hear anything?"

"As a matter of fact, I did. The trip was a success—or at least Genevieve said it was. I'm at the sheriff's office now, and

Steve has requested your presence, possibly because Iggy wouldn't tell his side of what happened until you arrive."

That sounded like him. "We'll be right there."

When I hung up, it was as if air could enter my lungs once more. "The gang is at Steve's office, and he has requested our presence."

Jaxson shoved back his chair. "What are we waiting for?"

We found everyone in the conference room. It wasn't a surprise that Iggy and Ruby were sitting in the middle of the table. I said nothing about them taking center stage again as Jaxson and I sat down.

"Who would like to begin?" Steve asked.

Genevieve raised her hand. "I will. Okay, so here is what happened. We all teleported inside Beth's house." She looked over at Hugo. "Yeah, Hugo stayed outside to keep guard, but he wasn't really needed since Beth never came home." She blew him a kiss.

"Go on," Steve said. By now he'd probably realized that Genevieve could be a tad long-winded.

"It took the three of us a while to locate the gems." She nodded to Iggy.

"That's where I came in. I was kind of scared that the spell might have worn off, but it didn't." Iggy glanced around, probably to see if he had the full attention of his audience. "Okay, I'll finish the story. It was really cool. Most of the places we looked were easy to open, like nightstands and stuff, because they didn't need a key. Naturally, nothing was in those places. Then we got to the desk drawer, and I had to do my thing, because it was locked."

"Which was what exactly?" I had seen him go through a

wall, and I hoped he'd had the chance to use that talent.

"I had to travel through wood!"

Even Steve's eyes widened at that announcement. "You teleported through wood?"

"Yippers. I don't know exactly how it worked, but I found myself inside without having to open the drawer."

Ruby nudged him and then lifted her chin. "I had to hold onto his tail while he did it. He feeds off my energy, you know."

Oh my, the egos were high today. "Then what?"

"I could sense when Iggy had found the bag, and I helped navigate him out," she said.

I couldn't be certain, but it looked like Iggy was glaring at Ruby for stealing the limelight.

He cleared his throat, if that was possible. "First, I have to say that while I was able to crawl right through the desk drawer, I might be scarred for life," he said.

What was he talking about? I did a quick scan of his body, and he looked okay. "What happened?"

"I stepped on a tack. That really hurt. And her drawer was filled with all sorts of other dangerous and sharp junk."

"As long as you aren't bleeding, you'll live. Tell us about what you found."

"I found the blue bag." Iggy looked at each person probably to see the admiration in their eyes. Oh, boy. He might be impossible to live with after this.

I'd have to speak with Genevieve to get a more unbiased opinion. "Did it have any gems inside?" I asked.

Steve lifted his yellow pad to reveal an evidence bag with a blue velvet drawstring pouch. "There were two rubies inside."

"Wow. So now what?"

"I may have evidence, but it was procured illegally, which means we can't do anything yet—other than send it into the lab to be tested. I want to see if this bag is the one that was inside the tombstone."

"I imagine Beth will notice it's missing at some point," Jaxson said.

"I'm hoping she does. I'm curious what she'll do. Until the test results come back, though, we can't do much. Even if it indicates that this bag was inside the monument, we can't arrest her since, as I said, the evidence was obtained without her permission."

"That kind of thing won't matter in a court of magical peers," I announced.

"Maybe not."

I guess that meant we were finished for the moment. "So we wait?"

"We wait, but I want to thank all of you for your help," Steve said.

Iggy waddled over to Steve. "What about Mrs. Hamilton's necklace?"

"What about it? It was stolen years ago—at least that is what the insurance company believes—or do you know something?"

"Nope. Just wondering." Iggy returned to me.

"Let us know if you find out anything else," I said to Steve.

"Of course."

I picked up Iggy and we left. "I could use some food. Anyone up for the Tiki Hut?" I asked.

"Sure," Iggy said. "I want to visit Aimee. I bet she'll want to hear all about my escapades and how I solved the crime."

"I'm sure." Or not. I hope he didn't brag too much. Besides, the case wasn't over yet.

THE NEXT FEW days were stressful while we waited for the test results on whether the thread Iggy found matched the bag in Beth's desk drawer. Steve had called in quite a few favors to get the results done quickly, but so far we hadn't heard anything. In case I haven't mentioned it before, I'm not very good at waiting.

The final result probably wouldn't matter all that much. If Steve learned the bag and the thread didn't match, I wasn't sure what he would do next. If they did match, he couldn't arrest her.

Just as I was about to polish off another bag of cookies to calm my jitters, my cell rang. "Jaxson, it's Steve."

My fiancé jumped up from the desk and came over. Iggy peeked his head out from under the sofa and crawled up the leg of the coffee table.

"Hey Steve, can I put you on speaker?"

"Sure."

"Did you get the test results?"

"No, but I had a visitor. It was Beth Langford."

My pulse shot up. "Really? What did she want?"

"You should be able to guess. She wanted to report a break-in."

That was an interesting twist. "She admitted that she had

a sack of rubies?"

"Yes, only she claimed there were six rubies, not the two that we found. She made certain to tell me that Mrs. Hamilton had given them to her, though I didn't ask her why. I then took some photos of the desk, but I'd like Iggy to take a look at them. Can you guys stop over?"

Iggy spun around. I couldn't recall the last time Steve specifically asked for my familiar's help. Maybe it was because now Steve could communicate with him. "Of course."

The three of us headed over. Jaxson had offered to carry Iggy, but he really seemed to like the independence of using the over-the-street monkey bridge. As usual, he beat us to the other side.

As soon as we crossed the street, Jaxson scooped Iggy up, and we then headed to Steve's office. I was almost happy that Pearl couldn't understand my familiar, because I'm sure Iggy would have bent her ear about his adventure.

"Steve's waiting for you in the conference room," she said. "And I put out a plate of cookies for you."

She was the best. "Thank you, thank you!"

Hugo, Genevieve, Andorra, Elizabeth, and Ruby were also there.

"Have a seat," Steve said. Once we sat down, he flipped through his yellow pad. "This morning, Beth Langford came in to report that some jewels had been stolen from her home."

"I still can't believe she admitted to having the rubies," I said.

"It wasn't as if she admitted to stealing them. Like I said, Beth claimed that Mrs. Hamilton had given them to her."

That was rich. "Before or after Ruby's host, Mrs. H, and

her husband, had accused her dad of stealing the necklace?"

"After."

I looked over at Ruby. "Do you know anything about this?"

"Nope. I only know about my host framing her dad."

"The lab results haven't come in yet about the thread and the bag, have they?" Jaxson asked.

"Not yet, I'm afraid."

I was more interested in what Steve was going to do about the *theft* at Beth's house. "You didn't say anything about having the items in question in your office, did you?"

He chuckled. "Hardly. What I did do, was check out her office. Turns out one of the windows was broken." He turned to Genevieve. "I'm assuming you didn't do this?"

"Why would I? We teleported inside. There was no need to break in."

He flashed her a quick smile. "I figured." Steve then produced a few photos and asked us to pass them around. "As you can see, the lock on the desk drawer looks like it was jimmied open."

"No one touched the lock," Iggy said with quite a lot of force. "I'm powerful. I was able to go through the desk drawer."

Too bad that ability had already worn off, much to his chagrin. "I'm guessing Beth tampered with the lock to make it look like a break-in?" I asked.

"That would be my guess."

"Did she have the gems appraised? If she didn't, she'd have a hard time convincing the insurance company to pay for her loss," I said.

"She said she never got around to it."

I huffed out a laugh. "Because she'd only recently acquired them."

"What's your next step?" Jaxson asked Steve.

"When the report comes back, if it says she is in possession of stolen property, I was hoping I could find something to arrest her for, even if it's a bogus charge. I figure I might be able to negotiate a deal of some sort."

That was a surprise. "If she's not in possession of the gems, what would be the charge? Lying to a police officer? Filing a false claim? We can't prove anything."

"I know what we can do," Genevieve said.

We all turned to her. "Tell us," Steve said.

"We could put the bag and gems back in her house—probably in a different spot, but make it easy for her to find. We'll see if she comes clean and says she's misplaced the gems, or if she tries to claim the loss on her insurance."

I didn't know the law, but I'm thinking that wouldn't work. "Or what if you arrest her, and say that Grant Stone felt so guilty about taking part in this theft that he turned Beth in?"

Steve dragged a hand down his jaw. "That might work, but you said if Beth were ever incarcerated she could melt the lock and escape."

"Yes. There is that," I said. "Breaking out of a jail is illegal, right?"

"Yes. What are you thinking?"

"We could have Hugo and Genevieve cloak themselves and even sit in the cell next to hers. The moment Beth breaks out, Hugo can do that immobilization thing he does.

Genevieve would call you and you'd…"

"I'd do what? Arrest her for real this time? She'd just escape again."

Even if she went to a prison for magical beings, they'd have to find a way to neutralize her talents. "Maybe, but we should take it one step at a time."

Pearl came rushing up to the conference room. She knocked and then pushed open the door. "Sorry to bother you, but the results of the thread matching came in." She handed the envelope to Steve.

My pulse soared. Iggy waddled over to him. I guess he thought he'd be the first to hear the verdict if he was the closest.

Steve unsealed the envelope and read the contents. He smiled. "It's a match."

"This proves that Beth Langford stole the gems that were hidden in the tombstone. Right?" Genevieve asked.

"Yes. Before I bring her in, I need to make sure we don't say or do anything we'll regret."

"Like I said, Hugo and I could return the pouch and leave it on or near her desk. We could see how she responds. I could be in and out in a flash." Genevieve looked over at Hugo and then nodded. "Hugo suggests that I wear one of those little camera things that I used last time. We can stay in her office and record what she does."

"None of what you find is admissible in our courts, but as you've all been saying, she won't be tried in our judicial system," Steve said.

Too bad Levy couldn't do a spell to remove her ability to heat things. He'd taken powers away from others before.

Before Steve told us what he was willing and able to do, Christine Thompson, one of Witch's Cove's most successful realtors came into the station.

"I wonder what she wants?" I mumbled.

"Let's see what my grandmother does."

We all watched as Pearl stood and escorted Christine into Steve's office. Pearl then came to the conference room.

"Sorry, again, but Christine is in the process of selling a house to Beth Langford."

Chapter Seventeen

STEVE STOOD. "THIS may be the break we've been waiting for. If you'll all excuse me. I will contact you when I figure out my next move. For now, let's sit tight and do nothing." He scooped up the envelope with the lab results.

Did he say to do nothing? He must not know who he was talking to. "Anyone want to do some brainstorming?" I asked once Steve was out of earshot.

"I have to get back to work, but you guys can use the back room," Elizabeth said.

"Works for me." I turned to Jaxson. "You want to come?"

"I'm game."

On the way out, we told Pearl we'd be at the Hex and Bones should Steve learn anything new.

We all reconvened in the back room, but I wasn't sure what I thought we'd accomplish by rehashing what we'd learned. Even if we figured out nothing, that was okay. I wasn't in the mood to go back to the office and wait for Steve's call.

"Glinda, I have a question," Jaxson said. "Suppose Steve agrees that Beth should be punished. We know she can't be tried in a non-magical court since she could escape, but how is this magical jail going to contain her?"

"I don't know, but of all the people who've been sent there, I haven't heard of anyone escaping. I'd be guessing that they either have persons of magic who remove the offender's powers, or there is some kind of dampening system that diffuses them."

"That makes sense," he said. "Whoever runs the prison must be really powerful."

I looked over at our two gargoyle shifters. "Have either of you heard of a gargoyle who could do that kind of thing?"

They both shook their heads. I suppose sitting on top of a church for years would prevent information from flowing.

Iggy made his way over to Ruby, which kind of surprised me since I thought his goal was to avoid her.

"If you can teleport, why didn't you leave the shelter?" Iggy asked. "Genevieve and Hugo can escape from anywhere."

Wow. I hadn't even thought of that, but maybe that was because at the time, I was unaware of her talents.

"I did leave. Many times. It got smelly and confining in there before they cleaned our cages."

"But we found you at the shelter," I interrupted.

"I know. The food's not the best, but at least there is food. One time I teleported to the supermarket, but I couldn't find the cat food. That place is really, really big."

I chuckled. "It is. Even if you found the canned tuna or canned chicken, I'm not sure even you could have opened the can."

"That's what I thought. I figured someone would eventually save me, which you did. Thank you."

"You are welcome." I returned my attention to the others. "I know we are supposed to wait for Steve to decide how to handle Beth Langford, but what about Mrs. Hamilton's stolen necklace?" I looked over at Ruby and back at the others. "Ruby here tells us that the necklace wasn't stolen, that it was a ploy to receive insurance money. That means it's still out there. Are we going to let that issue drop?" I asked.

"What can we do, Glinda?" Jaxson asked. "We don't know where it is, unless you think Chip knows."

I turned to Ruby. "You said Chip agreed to take the fall for stealing the necklace in return for Mrs. Hamilton looking out for Beth. Is that right?"

"That's what I heard, but I didn't stay around for the whole discussion. Mr. H told me to leave the room."

Interesting. "Is it possible the tombstone contained the necklace as well as the gems?" Genevieve asked.

I dragged my palms down my face. "I have no idea. I don't even know how we'd find out? You guys didn't find it at Beth's house, I take it?"

"Like we wouldn't have told you?" Iggy said with way too much sarcasm.

"I figured."

"Finding the necklace might be a waste of time, since we have no leads."

Before anyone else could comment further, Steve stepped into the room. "Pearl told me you'd be here. I have some news."

I motioned to the empty chair. I couldn't believe how my pulse had shot up. "Sit and tell us."

"I'm not sure how this will help us with the case, but as you heard, Beth Langford tried to purchase a house. She said it was for her dad."

Jaxson had suggested that Beth might have known that her dad had been framed and that his life had taken a severe downturn after being accused of the theft. She might have wanted to help make his life a bit easier. "That is really nice, but the money probably came from the sale of the gems," I said.

"That is why Christina came to me. Not everyone is aware that when you buy a house, you have to prove that you didn't procure the funds illegally. Usually, the money comes from the sale of another house, the sale of stocks, or if you've had the money in the bank for a while from having earned it. Beth tried to say that she'd inherited the money."

"That would be easy to prove or disprove," I said.

"Agreed. When Christine did some digging, she couldn't find any evidence of an inheritance. She'd heard about the stolen gems and thought the two might be connected."

I sighed. "Ah, the gossip tree in Witch's Cove is indeed alive and well."

He smiled. "While I have no definitive proof that the money came from the sale of the stones, it's looking more and more like Beth is our thief."

He doubted it? "Are you willing to have her tried in a court of her magical peers then? I imagine being in possession of at least two stones will be enough to convict her."

"I don't see that I have a choice. Before I turn her over to the other side, so to speak, I thought I would try one more thing. Unless Levy and his gang can take away her powers, I want to be absolutely sure she is a criminal."

He needed more proof? "What's your plan?"

"I will arrest her and tell her that Grant Stone came clean.

One of you suggested that, and I think it's a good idea. She might be willing to admit she stole the gems for a reduced sentence."

"Why would she bother?" I asked. "She knows you can't keep her in jail."

"All the more reason to admit guilt. She'd want to stop me from probing further. To her way of thinking, she has nothing to lose by admitting what she did. Beth knows we can't incarcerate her. I just hope she isn't aware of this other court."

"Let's hope," I said. If she was aware of it, it would complicate a lot of things.

Steve pointed a finger at Genevieve and Hugo. "That's where these two come in. I'd like to do as you suggested, Glinda. I'll ask Hugo and Genevieve to wait in the cell next to hers and see if she tries to escape. I know I'll have to replace the lock when this is done, but it will be one more thing to tell the courts—your court, not mine."

I liked it. "When do we start?"

He smiled. "Just as soon as I leave here." He turned to our two gargoyles. "Are you two up for that?"

Genevieve looked over at Hugo. "Absolutely. We'll go there now."

"You don't have"—He didn't get to finish his sentence before they left—"to go right now," Steve looked over at me. "Have you gotten used to them doing that?"

I chuckled. "Sometimes yes, sometimes, no. To be clear, if Beth doesn't sign a confession, you'll put her in the jail cell anyway, right?"

"Yes."

"Then once Beth tries to break out of jail, you'll escort her across the state to the world of magical justice."

"That's the plan," Steve said.

"May I suggest you ask Genevieve and Hugo to go with you when you escort Beth to the site. If they keep watch on her, she won't be able to melt her way out of there."

"That's a great idea. I will ask them. For now, I'd say the case is closed."

"What about Chip?" Jaxson asked.

"What about him?"

"If Ruby is to be believed, he was framed."

Steve looked over at the cat and then back at us. "I hardly think I can go to a judge and tell them a cat overheard Mr. and Mrs. Hamilton ask Chip Langford to admit he stole the necklace so they could get the insurance money."

Steve had a point. "I know you weren't sheriff back them, but maybe there is something in the transcripts that give Chip's side of the story."

"It's possible. I'll check it out. For now, go home and enjoy."

Jaxson and I stood. I should be feeling very satisfied that we'd solved another case, but I wasn't. Something was bothering me, but I couldn't figure out exactly what it was.

Just as he turned to leave, his cell rang. He answered it as he walked out of the door. Not that I was eavesdropping, but it sounded as if he was talking with his grandmother.

When he disconnected, he returned to the room. "You won't believe who else just walked into the office."

"Who?"

"Janette Schmidt, Mrs. Hamilton's daughter. And she has

the necklace with her."

No way! "Is she confessing to stealing it?"

"I won't know that until I speak with her. How about sitting tight? If I need you, Ruby, or Iggy, I'll call."

"Sure."

Once he was out of sight, I turned to Ruby. "How about teleporting to the jail and asking Genevieve to do a little eavesdropping on Steve and Mrs. Hamilton's daughter?"

"I can do that, but how about if I cloak myself and then listen in?"

I trusted Genevieve more, but Ruby probably knew Mrs. Hamilton's daughter better. "When was the last time you saw Mrs. Schmidt?"

"A long time ago. No, that's not true. Right before Mrs. H passed, she asked her daughter to visit."

"Was your host feeling guilty that the two of them hadn't had the best relationship?"

I think if Ruby could shrug, she would have. "I don't know."

"Is this daughter a witch?" Iggy asked.

"I think so. I wasn't a big fan of hers, so I kind of didn't talk much to her."

If Janette understood Ruby, most likely she was a witch, especially if her mother was. "Okay, fine. Go see what you can find out, but please don't show yourself or say anything. Steve will know that I was the one to ask you to spy on him. He'd never forgive me."

"Can I go with her?" Iggy asked.

"No. You know being cloaked takes energy."

Ruby sprawled onto her stomach. "I better not go then."

Really? "Why not?"

"It takes a lot of energy to teleport, and what if I can't keep cloaked either?"

That would be bad. "That's okay. Thanks for offering. I'm sure Steve will give us the scoop as soon as he can." When my phone rang, I jumped. "It's Steve," I told the group.

"Hey, that was quick. What did Janette say?" I asked him.

"Can you and the gang come over?"

That was cryptic. I wanted to ask why, but he must have his reasons. Most likely he wanted Ruby to confirm or deny what Janette said. "Sure."

"What did he say?" Jaxson asked.

"He wants all four of us to meet him at his office."

"Great." Jaxson scooped up Iggy.

I turned to Miss Pris. "Would you like me to carry you?"

"Yes, please."

After I spoke with Elizabeth and explained that I would return her familiar as soon as we were finished, we left. When we entered the sheriff's office, Pearl didn't say a word. She merely pointed to the conference room. Inside was a woman in her later years.

Jaxson pulled open the door with his free hand and motioned me in.

"Glinda, Jaxson, and gang. Please come in."

I almost stumbled. On the table was an open blue velvet box. Inside was the most bedazzling ruby and diamond necklace I'd ever seen. Whoa.

Chapter Eighteen

S TEVE INTRODUCED US to Janette Schmidt.

Ruby pranced up to the jewelry box. "Why do you have Mrs. H's necklace?"

"Because my mom gave it to me. Don't you remember when I came by before she passed?"

"I remember."

Janette turned to Steve. "You have to believe me. I had no idea that my mother and father had claimed this necklace had been stolen."

"They received insurance money for it. It was what helped restart the ruby mine."

Janette held up both hands. "I swear. My parents and I did not communicate after they didn't want my husband to take over the running of the mine."

"Did you know she'd written you out of her will?" Steve asked.

"I assumed she had, which was why I was so surprised when she asked that I return to Witch's Cove. I'd read that my dad had died, but she'd never told me. Like I said, things were not good between us."

Janette's posture was stiffer than a board, and her chin trembled a bit. I might not be able to read minds, but she seemed to be telling the truth.

Steve turned to Ruby. "What's your take?"

"What she said. Mrs. H always thought that Janette should be the first one to make up since she was the one to leave."

"I left because my parents didn't want my husband to help out."

Maybe her husband wasn't as qualified to run the mine as she thought.

"Mrs. Schmidt," Steve said. "Why bring the necklace in? And why today?"

"My husband and I were going to attend some fancy ball this weekend. I'd never worn the necklace mostly because it belonged to my mom, and secondly, it is worth a lot. I didn't want us to be robbed. It's why I stored it in a safety deposit box."

That could be true or not, but I bet Steve could find out, even though she no longer lived in Florida. Cops helped cops.

"Again, why bring it in?"

She opened her purse and pulled out a piece of paper. "When my mom gave me the necklace, I couldn't bear myself to look at it. She died shortly afterward. When I finally opened the box yesterday, I found this note from my mom. I'm ashamed to say that she explained everything—from insurance fraud to blackmailing someone named Chip Langford."

What? Blackmail? I really wanted to ask more questions, but I held my tongue. Jaxson reached over and squeezed my hand. That was his signal to me that I needed to let Steve do his thing.

Steve read the paper. He looked up. "If this was written by Mrs. Hamilton, it explains that the family business was in a lot of trouble financially and that Mr. Hamilton came up with the idea of pretending the valuable necklace was stolen."

I was glad that Steve didn't take Mrs. Schmidt's word for it that this was Mrs. Hamilton's handwriting.

"Can I see it?" Ruby asked. "I know her handwriting."

Steve's brows pinched. I don't blame him for not believing Ruby. "Iggy knows my handwriting, mostly because it isn't the neatest."

I kind of glared at him not to make a snarky comment. He merely lifted his head and looked away.

Steve motioned Ruby over. It took her less than fifteen seconds to say it was Mrs. Hamilton's. "She was always missing the letter T when she tried to cross it."

I was impressed with that.

"Okay then."

"What does it say about Chip being blackmailed?" Jaxson said.

"Mrs. Hamilton admitted that she and her husband basically forced Chip to admit he stole the necklace. He would do a few years in jail, but if he told anyone, then Mr. Hamilton would make sure that his ex-wife and daughter lost everything."

I whistled. "Not a nice man." Okay, I hadn't meant for that to slip out.

"No, my father was not. The mine was everything to him. Well, not totally, since he refused to take it over when it needed leadership."

Maybe she didn't realize how sick he was at the time.

Steve tapped the box. "This is property that the insurance company paid for."

She nodded. "Do with it what you need to. I honestly had no idea what my parents had done. When I read the note, I felt terrible for this Chip Langford person."

"Me, too," he said.

Janette turned to Ruby. "If it is any consolation, I always liked you."

I hope she wasn't going to ask if she could keep her.

"Thank you."

Good. We didn't need there to be a fight over who ended up with Ruby. I had the sense that this familiar was happy with Elizabeth.

Steve walked Mrs. Schmidt out and then returned. He picked up the jewelry box and closed the lid. "That was unexpected."

"That is an understatement," Jaxson said. "Are you going to show the note to the judge to see if Chip's record can be expunged?"

"I will. I also need to figure out what to do with the necklace. I imagine the insurance company will have a say in what needs to be done with it."

I imagine they'd sell it. After all, they paid for it. "What about Beth? I believe there are two gargoyles who are probably wondering where she is."

"I was about to arrest her when Janette Schmidt showed up."

I guess that meant we needed to get out of his way and let him do his thing. I pushed back my chair. "Good luck."

"Thanks."

AFTER WE RETURNED Ruby to the Hex and Bones, Iggy wanted to stay with her until Genevieve and Hugo returned. I thought that was rather odd since he said he couldn't stand her, but maybe Iggy had a hidden agenda. I'd have to ask him about it later. "Don't stay too late."

"Don't worry."

I didn't want to think about what that meant. Jaxson and I stopped at the Tiki Hut for a bite to eat. If we'd gone to the diner, Dolly would have picked our brains, and I certainly didn't need to mess up the investigation at this late stage.

Aunt Fern came over. "I haven't seen you in a while. How goes the tombstone case?"

"It's on-going, but our part is done, I think."

She pulled out a chair. "Tell me everything."

I looked around. "Can I fill you in later? I'm waiting to hear back about one piece of the puzzle. Then I can divulge all."

Aunt Fern smiled and pushed back her chair. "Of course. What can I get you guys?"

She rarely took orders, but we were special. I wanted coffee and a sandwich and Jaxson had coffee and a hamburger.

As soon as she disappeared into the kitchen, I leaned forward. "Didn't you think it really strange that Janette Schmidt would pick today to deliver the necklace?"

"Does it matter? We have the necklace that will give Chip the freedom he deserves."

Having been falsely accused of a crime, I can see why Jaxson would be anxious for Chip to be exonerated. "If Beth is tried in our magical court, Daniel makes a new tombstone for Mrs. Hamilton, and if Chip Langford is cleared of the theft, then I guess we won!"

"You are so right."

"How long do you think it will take Steve to bring Beth in?"

"I imagine not long," Jaxson said. "But I think he wants to tell her that Grant Stone turned her in. The only good a confession will do is to make the prosecutor's job in the magical court easier."

"True."

"If she tries to break out of jail, it will make it worse for her, but she won't know that," he said.

"I imagine so."

A server delivered our meal, and I dug in. "Steve still has those two rubies that Iggy and the gang found in Beth's desk drawer. I know we obtained them illegally, but I wonder what he'll do with them. They are worth quite a fortune."

"I don't know. I am not a lawyer," he said. "There will be money from the sale of the rest of the jewels, too. I imagine the funds are in Beth's account if she tried to pay for a house for her dad."

"I should have gotten an accounting degree or maybe a law degree. They'd come in handy. Too bad, I would have been bored out of my mind."

Jaxson reached across the table and rubbed my arm. "It's out of our hands. Let's enjoy our meal, and then maybe take a walk on the beach."

I smiled. "I like the way you think."

After we finished eating, we spent an hour enjoying the

Gulf of Mexico coastline. I loved the feel of the sand on my feet and the salty smell of the sea. Seagulls were buzzing overhead, and I couldn't help but try to spot a particular white bird with black-tipped wings. I failed, but the journey was fun.

After my legs didn't want to walk anymore, we went back to my place to clean up. Sand always managed to find its way into every crevice. Afterward, we planned to go back to the office. Rihanna would have returned from school, and I wanted to fill her in on what had happened.

I'd just finished cleaning my feet when Genevieve popped in—as in just appeared. I'd given up trying to train her to knock on the door.

"This is a surprise. I thought you were at the jail."

"I was. Hugo is there now—with Beth. If she tries to escape, he can handle it. I just wanted to fill you in, and then I'll go back."

"Great. Have a seat. Tell us what happened."

"You'll have to ask Steve what he did, but as soon as Beth showed up, Hugo cloaked himself, but I remained visible. I thought I might be able to get her to talk."

That sounded promising. "What did she say?"

"Well, at first she was furious. No one likes to get caught," Genevieve said.

"She admitted to stealing the tombstone?"

"No, but I didn't bring it up either. She did mumble something about getting back at Grant Stone."

That was good news. "Steve must have revealed his source."

Genevieve tittered like only she could. "I really wanted to

174

tell her that I told Steve, but I thought he'd be mad."

"Then what?" Jaxson asked.

"When I left, she was standing at the cell bars, probably trying to figure out how to get out."

"Even if she melts the iron bars, she can't think she could get past Steve." I sucked in a breath. "You don't think she can teleport, do you?"

"I don't think so. If she could have, she'd be long gone."

That was a relief. "So now what?"

"I'll go back."

"Wait a minute. If you were in the cell and then disappeared, what is Beth going to think?"

Genevieve's mouth dropped open. "Whoops. I might have to have Hugo do something to her memory."

"You need to think before you act," Jaxson said. "Hugo might not always be there to correct things."

"I know. I'll try harder."

Before we could continue with the lecture on responsibility, she left. I hoped she didn't mess up Steve's plan—not that we needed Beth to break out of jail to convict her of the theft.

When we returned to the office, Rihanna had just rolled in, and we filled her in.

"Wow. I attend three classes, and you guys solve the case."

That was an exaggeration. "Not us personally. The others did the heavy lifting."

"Knock, knock," Steve said as he opened the office door.

"Hey, come in."

Steve stepped inside. "I wanted to fill you in on Beth."

"Genevieve kind of did."

That comment resulted in a long discussion on whether

he could trust her ever again.

I was glad he wasn't going to dismiss her right away. He needed her to help transport the prisoner across the state.

"Tell us about Beth's arrest," Jaxson said.

"It went according to plan. I told her that Grant Stone turned her in. I thought she'd question why, but she was so mad that she didn't ask."

"Did you get her to confess?"

"I did, but I don't think she believed it would make a difference. She probably knew she could get out of any jail."

"Wait until she meets Hugo," I said.

"That's what I'm hoping."

"When are you taking her to stand trial?" Jaxson asked.

"I'll call over there tomorrow and set it up."

"You are taking Hugo and Genevieve, right?" I asked.

"I am. I don't need her reaching through the grate in the police car and heating my head to fry my brains."

I hoped he was kidding. "Good luck."

"And Chip Langford?" Jaxson asked.

He smiled. "Don't worry. I've sent the information to the judge. As soon as the paperwork comes through, I will give him the good news."

"Thank you," Jaxson said.

Steve stood. "I'll be in touch."

Chapter Nineteen

One week later

A KNOCK SOUNDED on our office door, and I glanced over at Jaxson. Usually people just came in. We even had a sign on the door that said to enter.

I walked over to the door and pulled it open. "Mr. Langford, this is a surprise."

"May I come in?"

"Of course." I motioned him inside.

Jaxson stood, went over to him, and shook Chip's hand. "I hope you come with good news."

"I do, and I wanted to thank you both."

Jaxson motioned for him to have a seat. "Tell us."

"The sheriff first showed me the note that Mrs. Hamilton had written that proved I was blackmailed. Even after Mr. Hamilton died, I never thought I'd get my record erased. I still can't believe it. You said that happened to you?" he asked Jaxson.

"Yes. It took a long time for it to sink in. I could have let the anger take over my life for having spent three years in jail, but now that I'm out, I'm not sure I'd trade that time for anything."

I'd never heard Jaxson talk about his time there. "How

so?"

"I learned to deal with my past a little better. I don't want to be a downer, but you come to terms with where your life had been and what you plan to do once you get out."

"I totally agree," Chip said. "I just wanted my family back, and I was willing to do anything. My wife has moved on, and I can't blame her, but I was able to spend time with Beth."

I hissed in a breath. "I am sorry that she was caught up in this."

He dipped his chin. "I know. You and me both, but Beth was always an angry girl. She had talents, but never learned how to harness them for good. I knew she wanted someone to pay for what happened to me, but I told her to let it go."

"She couldn't though," I said.

"No. Beth made the decision she did, and I'm sorry for both of us, but she'll eventually serve her time. She's young. All I can hope for is that she turns her life around."

I had to assume he knew where she was being tried and what kind of place it was.

He stood. "Mr. Sharpe said that the new tombstone will be ready soon."

"I'm glad. Are you going to try to go back to real estate?" I asked.

"No. I've actually found managing the cemetery to be rather peaceful. The tenants are all very well behaved."

I liked his attitude. "I'm happy for you."

We thanked him for stopping by and telling us, and then we wished him good luck. Chip Langford was a nice man.

A few minutes after he left, Iggy barged through the cat

door. "Victory is near."

I had no idea what he was talking about. "Victory over what?"

"Why, over Tippy of course. It was so cool. I wanted to show Ruby our beach, so she teleported across the street while I went over on the monkey bridge."

Oh, no. "Iggy, Ruby can't be doing that in the light of day. What if someone saw her?"

"So what if they did? We could be known as the town of the magical cat."

I groaned. "Seriously? I thought you didn't like Ruby. Do you want her to be famous?" And bring thousands into town to see her teleport? "I'm betting it isn't good for her health to move around like that too often."

"I guess not." He dropped onto his stomach.

Darn. "Tell me about this victory over Tippy."

He lifted up. "Okay, so we were on the beach near some sea oats when I spotted him overhead. I told Ruby to be careful, that Tippy might poop on her."

"How did she react?" If I recall, Aimee, his one-time girlfriend, didn't seem to mind seagulls.

"She howled, I guess to attract his attention. Then when Tippy was nose-diving us, Ruby grabbed my tail, and we teleported out of there. It was the coolest thing ever. Okay, I know I've time traveled before, but this was equally as cool."

I wanted to lecture him about the dangers of doing that too often, but I couldn't dampen his joy. "That's great. Are you and Ruby best friends now?"

"She's a girl. Hugo and I are buddies, as are me and Jaxson, but I suppose if Ruby can help me become a better man, I might keep her around."

I cracked up. Life around my familiar was never dull.

What's next? Glinda and Jaxson are spending Christmas with his parents. She plans to relax and enjoy herself. Too bad someone drops dead at the holiday party. Check out THE PINK CHRISTMAS COOKIE CAPER.

Buy on Amazon or read for FREE on Kindle Unlimited

Don't forget to sign up for my Cozy Mystery newsletter *to learn about my discounts and upcoming releases. If you prefer to only receive notices regarding my releases, follow me on BookBub.*
http://smarturl.it/VellaDayNL
bookbub.com/authors/vella-day

Here is a sneak peak of book 17:
THE PINK CHRISTMAS COOKIE CAPER

"I'M NERVOUS," I told my fiancé, Jaxson Harrison, as he turned into his parents' subdivision in Magnolia, Florida.

"Why?"

"I haven't seen your parents in what? Ten years? The last time, I was Drake's best friend."

"And now you're my fiancée. There's nothing to worry about."

"I hope so, but it will be my first Christmas not spending it with my parents. It's going to feel a bit, I don't know, strange."

He glanced over at me. "Your folks have Rihanna and your Aunt Fern to keep them company on Christmas day. We'll be back in two days. We can celebrate Christmas with them then."

"I know. And Rihanna's mom is going to be there, too, so they will have plenty of family love on Christmas morning."

I was being selfish wanting to be with my folks, as well as with Jaxson, on that special day, but celebrating the evening of the twenty-sixth would be good enough. Last year, he and his brother, Drake, had spent the holidays with their parents, and I missed both of them. This year, we decided to split our time between the two families so that we could be together.

By the way, I'm Glinda Goodall, a not very powerful witch, who runs the Pink Iguana Sleuths Company with Jaxson. Quite often, some type of magic is involved in a crime, and when that happens, the sheriff calls on us to help solve the mystery. Thankfully, this month, nothing had been stolen nor had anyone been murdered, which meant we were free to travel.

Jaxson ran a quick hand over my arm. "You know, it will be nice to relax and not have to hunt down a murderer or try to find some stolen object for a change. Think about it. If we're here, we won't be tempted to find trouble."

"That's true." The problem was that I kind of liked having something to do. I wasn't an idle hands type of person.

Jaxson pulled into the driveway and parked. "I see Drake and Andorra beat us here." He pulled in next to their vehicle.

I was excited to spend time with my two good friends. I'd only reunited with Andorra, a high school acquaintance, a few months ago, but we'd bonded quickly, partly because we worked together to solve a murder—a pretty commonplace occurrence for me. As for Drake, we'd been inseparable since middle school. But then I met Jaxson, and shall we say, the rest is history.

The outside of the Harrison's brick home was decorated with Christmas lights—a lot of Christmas lights—and lawn ornaments, which included a Santa and sleigh on top of the roof. A second set of illuminated reindeers littered the lawn, as did some playful elves. I couldn't wait until it was dark. The visual effect would be stunning.

Jaxson cut the engine. "Remember, my mom's name is Maddy and my dad—"

"Yes, is Eugene. I remember." We'd been over this a few times. Maybe he was anxious, too.

Iggy, my familiar, who had ridden over on my lap, lifted his head. "I bet Mrs. Harrison won't recognize me.

"Why is that?" It wasn't as if there were a lot of pink

iguanas—at least in Florida.

"I'm so big now."

"That's true." I turned to Jaxson. "I hadn't thought of it, but I wonder if Drake will want your folks to meet Hugo." That was Andorra's familiar, though it would be harder to explain what looked like a grown man to her boyfriend's parents.

"Hugo might come?" Iggy asked.

The hope in his voice tore at my soul. Hugo was Iggy's best friend. Andorra never mentioned that Hugo might be there, but perhaps she could call the Hex and Bones Apothecary, the town's occult store that her grandmother owned, and ask him to stop by. After all, the gargoyle shifter could teleport. "We'll see, but no promises."

"Okay," he said, not sounding all that optimistic.

I twisted toward Jaxson. "Did Drake say anything about why he invited Andorra? I mean, asking a girlfriend for Christmas implies something might happen." As in, was he going to ask her to marry him?

Jaxson chuckled. "I have no idea, and even if I did, I wouldn't tell you." He tapped my nose and then pushed open the door.

"Fine, don't tell me." I placed Iggy in my purse and then eased out of the truck. The back seat held presents and our suitcases. "Should we take all of this inside now?"

"Let's leave everything in the truck for now."

My nerves shot up, which was irrational. I'd only gained about twenty pounds since high school, but I was a bit self-conscious about it.

Jaxson knocked and then opened the door. "Hello?"

"Is that you, Jaxson?" a female voice called.

Was his mother expecting someone else? As if a beehive had been poked, Drake, Andorra, and an older couple emerged from another room—the den or the kitchen perhaps? I couldn't guess which room was in the back, because the inside of the house looked like a Christmas showroom. Santas, elves, stockings hung with care over the fireplace, giant candy canes, and three-feet tall toy soldiers filled every nook and cranny. And here, I thought my mom was a fanatic because of her love of the movie, *The Wizard of Oz*, but she paled in comparison to Jaxson's mother.

"Hi, Mom." Jaxson hugged her.

She leaned back and ran her gaze up and down his body. "You look…wonderful. And happy." Maddy Harrison turned to me. "Oh, Glinda, it's wonderful to see you again. Thank you for giving my son his glow." She grinned.

Before I could respond to that, I found myself in a super human bear hug. "You, too, Mrs. H."

"She's squishing me!" That plea came from Iggy.

As graciously as I could, I leaned back. "Iggy's in my bag."

"Oh, I am so sorry. Can I see him?"

I was pleased she remembered that Iggy was a male. "Sure."

I lifted him out, and she squealed. "He's as cute as I remember. May I hold him?"

People usually didn't make that request. "Iggy? What do you say?"

"Tell her not to hold me too tight."

I handed him to her. "Be gentle."

Maddy immediately dragged her hand lightly over his

184

dorsal crest. I waited for him to complain, but he seemed to like it. Maybe we'd get through this vacation without drama after all.

His dad patted Jaxson on the back and then faced me. "Glinda, Goodall. Aren't you a sight for sore eyes."

I held out my hand, but he hugged me instead. "Nice to see you again, too."

His skin was a bit more sallow than I remember, but that could be because he'd been ill a few months ago.

As for Jaxson's mom, she was still a beauty—tall, fit, with shoulder length salt and pepper hair, and a perfect smile that lit up the room.

"Where are my manners? You guys must be tired. Come sit down. Can I get you anything to drink?"

If she hadn't sounded like she wanted to fix us something, I would have said no. "Some coffee would be great."

"Perfect. And for you, darling?"

"The same, but Glinda likes it with cream and sugar."

"No problem. I'll be right back." She handed Iggy back to me. I would have asked if he was okay, but he seemed to have lasered his focus on the parrot in the cage.

I hoped that wouldn't be a problem. Iggy had issues with birds.

"They have a parrot!" Iggy said in a tone that sounded like more like a growl.

I remember when they took in Pete. "I forgot about him," I whispered, "but he's not a seagull. And he's in a cage, so you don't have worry." Iggy had an ongoing war with a local seagull he'd named Tippy. "Tippy is white and this bird is red with blue wings. They don't look anything alike."

"Maybe, but I'm not taking any chances," he said.

I had no idea what he meant by that. I turned to Jaxson.

I hoped he wouldn't be a problem for Iggy. Right now, I wanted to concentrate on his folks.

I walked over to the seating area in the living room, where my friends had parked themselves, probably so that I could spend a moment with Jaxson's loving folks.

"Hey, guys," I said.

Andorra and Drake stood and gave me a hug. "Good ride over?" Drake asked.

I smiled. "Uneventfully good."

Eugene motioned we take the sofa, while he, Andorra and Drake sat on large comfy chairs that were more or less in front of the fully decorated Christmas tree. Underneath, presents were piled high. Oh, my.

His dad leaned forward. "Glinda, in case you forgot, Maddy still goes overboard on everything." He swung his arm around the room. "Later this afternoon, we are having a neighborhood Christmas party, so be prepared for more overload."

I couldn't imagine what that meant if it was more over-the-top than her decorated home. "I'm sure it will be fun to meet all of your neighbors."

Jaxson's mom returned with our drinks. She set the tray down on the large wooden coffee table and then took the chair next to her husband. "I heard Eugene warn you about our small get together. It's just some neighbors and a few of the city council members that the boy's dad works with."

I thought their father was retired. Jaxson needed to do a better job of updating me.

"So, Glinda, how are your folks, and what have you been doing since high school?" Maddy asked. "I only know what Drake and Jaxson tell me. And you know boys. They don't say much."

I told them about my one year teaching, and finally how I waitressed at my aunt's restaurant, which was when Jaxson was accused of murder. "Just your usual upbringing." I smiled.

"I will be eternally grateful for you believing in Jaxson and helping him prove he was framed."

"I'm the lucky one," I said as I squeezed Jaxson's hand.

Okay, we were getting a little sappy here, but it was nice to see how much the Harrisons adored their sons. We spent the next hour talking about Drake's plans for his cheese and wine shop and then whether Andorra planned to take over the occult store when her grandmother retired.

"Probably. Elizabeth and I make a good team."

When there was no mention of Hugo, I sensed no one had told the Harrison's about him or his gargoyle shifting girlfriend.

Maddy stood. "The guests will be arriving in an hour. I bet you four would like to freshen up. Andorra, can you show Glinda to your room?"

"Sure."

"Jaxson," Maddy said. "You'll bunk with Drake in his room."

"Great." Jaxson turned to me. "I'll get the luggage and deliver it to your room."

Between the suitcases and the presents, he'd need help. "I can carry a few things."

Drake held up a hand. "We got this. You two get ready."

That was code for him wanting to chat with Jaxson about something—alone.

"Come on, Glinda," Andorra said.

I followed her into a room that was definitely all male. It had a twin bed covered with a plaid bedspread, and next to it was a cot. I stepped over to the desk. "She kept Jaxson's wrestling trophies from high school?"

I couldn't recall when his parents had moved from Witch's Cove to Magnolia, but I think it was after Jaxson had been arrested for a theft he was later cleared of.

"She's nostalgic. It's sweet and creepy at the same time. It's the same with Drake's room. He tried to toss some of his stuff when he came home the last time, but his mom said it kept her sons close to have their trophies and such in the house."

That was a little sad. Iggy wiggled, and I placed him on the cot. "Maybe you should stay in here during the party," I told him. "We don't need you to be trampled on."

"You mean attacked by that bird. It's a parrot, yet it hasn't said anything. What's up with that? Do you think he can't talk, like Hugo?"

"I have no idea."

Jaxson came in with my suitcase. "Mom said the get together is a casual affair, but that means wear a dress."

I smiled. "Gotcha."

"Oh, and she has sandwiches in the kitchen. This Christmas affair is a dessert party, and I told her we were hungry for real food."

I grinned. He was hungry for real food. Me? I had a sweet tooth. "I'll be right out as soon as I jump in the shower."

"I'm good. I just need to change," Andorra said.

As I dashed into the attached bath, Iggy asked Andorra if Hugo could visit. I didn't hear her response, but it would be better if she let him down instead of me.

I quickly cleaned up. When I stepped into the bedroom with a towel wrapped around me, Andorra had changed into a lovely sapphire blue dress.

"You look really nice," I said.

She smiled. "Thanks. I'm going to head to the kitchen. I'm starving."

"I hear ya. Be right out."

In short order, I changed and joined everyone. Not only was there a plate of delicious looking sandwiches on the counter, a large plate of brownies topped with pink frosting and another plate of sugar cookies with pink frosting were on display, too.

"Is someone else a pink fan?" I hadn't seen anything else pink in the house. Red and green had dominated the Christmas theme.

Jaxson chuckled "No, this is for you. It's partially my fault. I might have mentioned a time or two that your favorite color is pink. Mom just wanted to make you feel at home, and as usual, she went a little overboard."

"I think it's sweet." I grabbed a sandwich and a bottle of water and sat on the stool at the island.

Drake moaned. "I forgot how good Magnolia Deli's roast beef sandwiches are."

He was right. The meat was cooked to perfection. For the next fifteen minutes, we chowed down and said little. The kitchen was in the rear of the house in a separate room, but the distinctive doorbell chime filtered back to us.

Jaxson tossed his napkin on his place, picked it up, and stood. "Showtime!"

This was going to be fun.

Buy On Amazon

THE END

A WITCH'S COVE MYSTERY (Paranormal Cozy Mystery)
PINK Is The New Black (book 1)
A PINK Potion Gone Wrong (book 2)
The Mystery of the PINK Aura (book 3)
Box Set (books 1-3)
Sleuthing In The PINK (book 4)
Not in The PINK (book 5)
Gone in the PINK of an Eye (book 6)
Box Set (books 4-6)
The PINK Pumpkin Party (book 7)
Mistletoe with a PINK Bow (book 8)
The Magical PINK Pendant (book 9)
The Poisoned PINK Punch (book 10)
PINK Smoke and Mirrors (book 11)
Broomsticks and PINK Gumdrops (book 12)
Knotted Up In PINK Yarn (book 13)
Ghosts and PINK Candles (book 14)
Pilfered PINK Pearls (book 15)
The Case of the Stolen PINK Tombstone (book 16)
The PINK Christmas Cookie Caper (book 17)
Pink Moon Rising (book 18)

SILVER LAKE SERIES (3 OF THEM)
(1). **HIDDEN REALMS OF SILVER LAKE** (Paranormal
Romance)
Awakened By Flames (book 1)
Seduced By Flames (book 2)
Kissed By Flames (book 3)
Destiny In Flames (book 4)
Box Set (books 1-4)

Passionate Flames (book 5)

Ignited By Flames (book 6)

Touched By Flames (book 7)

Box Set (books 5-7)

Bound By Flames (book 8)

Fueled By Flames (book 9)

Scorched By Flames (book 10)

(2). **FOUR SISTERS OF FATE: HIDDEN REALMS OF SILVER LAKE** (Paranormal Romance)

Poppy (book 1)

Primrose (book 2)

Acacia (book 3)

Magnolia (book 4)

Box Set (books 1-4)

Jace (book 5)

Tanner (book 6)

(3). **WERES AND WITCHES OF SILVER LAKE**

(Paranormal Romance)

A Magical Shift (book 1)

Catching Her Bear (book 2)

Surge of Magic (book 3)

The Bear's Forbidden Wolf (book 4)

Her Reluctant Bear (book 5)

Freeing His Tiger (book 6)

Protecting His Wolf (book 7)

Waking His Bear (book 8)

Melting Her Wolf's Heart (book 9)

Her Wolf's Guarded Heart (book 10)

His Rogue Bear (book 11)

Box Set (books 1-4)
Box Set (books 5-8)
Reawakening Their Bears (book 12)

OTHER PARANORMAL SERIES
PACK WARS (Paranormal Romance)
Training Their Mate (book 1)
Claiming Their Mate (book 2)
Rescuing Their Virgin Mate (book 3)
Box Set (books 1-3)
Loving Their Vixen Mate (book 4)
Fighting For Their Mate (book 5)
Enticing Their Mate (book 6)
Box Set (books 1-4)
Complete Box Set (books 1-6)

HIDDEN HILLS SHIFTERS (Paranormal Romance)
An Unexpected Diversion (book 1)
Bare Instincts (book 2)
Shifting Destinies (book 3)
Embracing Fate (book 4)
Promises Unbroken (book 5)
Bare 'N Dirty (book 6)
Hidden Hills Shifters Complete Box Set (books 1-6)

CONTEMPORARY SERIES
MONTANA PROMISES (Full length contemporary
Romance)
Promises of Mercy (book 1)
Foundations For Three (book 2)
Montana Fire (book 3)

Montana Promises Box Set (books 1-3)
Hart To Hart (Book 4)
Burning Seduction (Book 5)
Montana Promises Complete Box Set (books 1-5)

ROCK HARD, MONTANA (contemporary romance
novellas)
Montana Desire (book 1)
Awakening Passions (book 2)

PLEDGED TO PROTECT (contemporary romantic
suspense)
From Panic To Passion (book 1)
From Danger To Desire (book 2)
From Terror To Temptation (book 3)
Pledged To Protect Box Set (books 1-3)

BURIED SERIES (contemporary romantic suspense)
Buried Alive (book 1)
Buried Secrets (book 2)
Buried Deep (book 3)
The Buried Series Complete Box Set (books 1-3)

A NASH MYSTERY (Contemporary Romance)
Sidearms and Silk(book 1)
Black Ops and Lingerie(book 2)
A Nash Mystery Box Set (books 1-2)

STARTER SETS (Romance)
Contemporary
Paranormal

Author Bio

Love it HOT and STEAMY? Sign up for my newsletter and receive MONTANA DESIRE for FREE. smarturl.it/o4cz93?IQid=MLite

OR Are you a fan of quirky PARANORMAL COZY MYSTERIES? Sign up for this newsletter. smarturl.it/CozyNL

Not only do I love to read, write, and dream, I'm an extrovert. I enjoy being around people and am always trying to understand what makes them tick. Not only must my romance books have a happily ever after, I need characters I can relate to. My men are wonderful, dynamic, smart, strong, and the best lovers in the world (of course).

My Paranormal Cozy Mysteries are where I let my imagination run wild with witches and a talking pink iguana who believes he's a real sleuth.

I believe I am the luckiest woman. I do what I love and I have a wonderful, supportive husband, who happens to be hot!

Fun facts about me

(1) I'm a math nerd who loves spreadsheets. Give me numbers and I'll find a pattern.

(2) I live on a Costa Rica beach!

(3) I also like to exercise. Yes, I know I'm odd.

I love hearing from readers either on FB or via email (hint, hint).

Social Media Sites

Website: www.velladay.com
FB: facebook.com/vella.day.90
Twitter: @velladay4
Gmail: velladayauthor@gmail.com

Printed in Great Britain
by Amazon